A CONFLUENCE OF OBSIDIAN

LYDIA M. HAWKE

**Published by Michem Publishing,
Canada**

A Confluence of Obsidian

October 1, 2025

Cover design by Deranged Doctor Design
Interior design by AuthorTree

ISBN: 978-1-989457-39-9
MICHEM PUBLISHING

Chapter 1

By the time the Mage message arrived, we were beginning to give up hope.

None of us said so, of course, but the knowledge was there. It sat between us, weighed us down, dogged our every footstep, had coffee with us in the morning and hot chocolate by the fire after dinner, and grew stronger with every passing day.

Six of them.

Six days since we'd returned from our triumph over the Mages at the Citadelle to find the monastery's front door hanging from a single hinge, a smear of crimson across the front entrance floor, and Talia gone. The enormity of that night's discovery hit me like a gut punch every time I remembered it …

Including now.

I looked down at the plain, white square of paper resting on the floor from which Sister Lise had silently cleaned the blood less than a week ago, and then at the heavy wooden door that had crashed open as I'd raced down the stairs. If my heart hadn't already been pounding from Methuselah's sudden appearance at my bedside, it certainly would have been now.

His words still echoed in my brain.

"They're coming."

It would have been a hell of a way to wake up, if I'd been sleeping.

I had not been.

Snow swirled into the entry from the dark, silent night beyond, pushed by the icy fingers of a wind not nearly strong enough to have torn open the monastery's weighty door. Footsteps thudded down the stairs in the hall behind me, heralding the arrival of the Ursuline nuns and Phoenix. From further away came the faint *squeakity-squeak* of the wheels on Sister Colette's rolling walker.

The troops joined me, three on one side and two on the other, forming a half-circle around the paper on the floor as winter plastered their nightgowns and robes against their legs —except for Phoenix, of course, who had given up on the monastery's ancient heating system and taken to sleeping in sweatpants and a hoodie.

Methuselah was nowhere to be seen.

"*Tabarnak*," muttered Sister Colette. "Couldn't they have just slipped it *under* the door?"

"And not make a scene of some kind?" Sister Simonne snorted as she wrapped her thin dressing gown tighter around herself. She held it in place with both arms as she shivered. "I don't think Mages know how to operate like that."

"Is that who it's from?" demanded Phoenix to my immediate left. "It's about freaking time!"

She dived toward the paper, but Sister Bernadette and I both caught hold of her arms and pulled her back.

"Stop!" Sister Bernadette barked. "If it *is* from them, it might be dangerous."

"Who else *could* it be from?" Sister Lise asked, gesturing at the open door. "There's no one outside, and there are no footprints on the porch, and even if there were, there's no way to open the door from there."

"She's right," Sister Bernadette said, meeting my gaze across Phoenix's bright pink head.

I nodded agreement. The lack of a handle on the exterior of the door was a leftover from the monastery's cloistered days, when visitors were actively discouraged. No one could have opened it without—

Phoenix tugged her arm free of my grip and waved it at the paper still lying on the floor.

"Who cares about the door?" she snarled. "If that's a message from the Mages, it'll be about Talia. You know, our *friend?*"

I did know. I knew all too well. I also knew that, if the consortium really had sent it, it was just as likely to be a trap as a message. Either way, however, we could hardly leave it lying on the floor while we all stared at it and slowly froze to death in the entry.

I met Sister Bernadette's gaze again. A dozen swift, unspoken questions and answers passed between me and the head of the Ursuline nuns who had taken in me and Phoenix —and who, as one of the Obsidian Sisterhood who had protected Methuselah and the powerful stones he'd brought to Earth millennia ago, understood exactly what was at stake here.

"Are you sure?" her eyes asked.

"Do I have a choice? We can't leave it where it is, and we need to know."

"We do know."

"I know. But ..."

The nun's gaze flicked briefly toward the ceiling and the second floor where Methuselah would still be in hiding—or maybe he'd reverted to his child again and retreated to his safe place on the deserted, unused third floor. Whichever it was— and no matter how powerful he might still be—I did not want him anywhere near this. I gave a tiny shake of my head, and understanding flashed across Sister Bernadette's face before she turned grim.

"Be careful," her expression said, as she steered a protesting Phoenix toward the living room doorway.

I waited as sisters Lise, Simonne, and Colette fell back to join them—not that being in the next room would offer them much protection, since all their heads still poked through the doorway—and then turned my attention to the paper. Slowly, cautiously, I squatted beside it, took a deep breath, and, leaning as far away from it as I could without toppling, lifted one corner from the floor.

Nothing happened.

The breath I'd taken gusted from me, drowned out by the collective exhale from the living room doorway behind me. I picked up the paper in its entirety and, still squatting, examined it. It was an envelope, devoid of writing or marks of any kind on the front, and bearing a wax seal on the reverse side that had rested on the floor. I brushed a fingertip against the wax. Again, nothing.

I pushed back up to my feet, envelope in hand, then glanced over my shoulder to be sure the others had remained at a distance. They had, and deep concern was etched across all their faces. Phoenix peeked between sisters Lise and Colette with Sister Bernadette's hand resting protectively—preventively?—on her shoulder.

Squaring my shoulders and keeping my back to my companions—because if this thing exploded, I wanted to be sure I took the brunt of it—I slid one finger beneath the envelope's flap.

And oh, I took the brunt of it, all right.

In spades.

THE ENVELOPE DIDN'T EXPLODE, EXACTLY, BUT HAVING IT burst into a ball of flames was a close second. Especially when those flames engulfed both my hands the instant the wax seal broke.

I reacted instinctively, throwing the roiling, crimson sphere away from me, toward the door I'd just closed, but I wasn't fast enough. Searing pain flashed across my fingertips and palms, and tears of agony blinded me. I ignored both, yelling at the others to stay back as I tried to keep myself between them and the inferno engulfing the entry. Not because I thought of myself as any more heroic than any of them, but because when Methuselah had come into my room and those eyes filled with galaxies had stared into mine, I hadn't hesitated.

"They're coming," he'd whispered.

The stone beneath my pillow had been in my hand before he'd finished speaking. I wanted it there now, but skin sloughed off my fingers when I tried to force them into my pocket—damn my decision to get dressed before coming downstairs.

But the stone didn't need me to hold it for it to work its magick. Already, strands of its spiderwebs slipped along my veins, reaching for my injured hands. They skimmed over the palms and wrapped around my fingers, binding my skin, cooling it, easing its pain—

And then they snaked out of me toward the fire, fury backing their intent.

My fury.

I squeezed my hands into fists, reigniting the discomfort in them, using it as a focal point ... an anchor. The stone bucked against my mental hold on it. I staggered under its sudden weight but refused to drop to my knees or reach to ground myself against the floor. Control teetered back and forth between us, and then—

Then the fire merged into the figure of a Mage. Specifically that of Ronald Drummond.

CHAPTER 2

I knew he wasn't real, of course—or rather, I hoped to hell and back that he wasn't—but that didn't stop me from caving to instinct and throwing myself to the floor, injuries forgotten and stone in one hand as I slammed the other against the snow-covered tiles.

A very distant part of me noted the icy shock with a surprised little *huh*—as in, *how can the fire have burned me and not melted the snow?* But the greater part of me was more concerned with how Drummond's eyes—even though he wasn't really here—tracked my movement, because again, *how?*

"Listen carefully," his image said, the gaze boring into mine as he stared down his nose at me and delivered his one-way message with his trademark haughty arrogance, *"because I will only say this once. You have one week to deliver the alien to us, along with the remaining stone that is in your possession. One week, and one week only. After that, we send one body part per day until you comply. If you continue to defy us and your friend doesn't survive, we will take another of you. And then another. And then another. You cannot win, Ms. Barrett. You cannot defeat us. We'll send further instructions when we're ready, and be warned—there will be no negotiation."*

From fire to warning, it was all over in less than a minute. Even if Drummond had actually been present, even if he'd been able to hear me, I would have had no time to respond, no time to react, no time to so much as blink before the fire flared again. Heat washed over me as I buried my face in the crook of my arm. Then, like the Mage it had brought, the fire was gone, taking the envelope and wax seal with it.

I stared at the tiny pyramid of ash sitting on the floor in front of me in the snow, which still hadn't melted. At my outstretched hand, claw-like against the tile I'd tried to ground myself to. At—

Slippered feet entered my peripheral vision, the ankles above them pale and blue-veined. Strong, capable hands slipped beneath my arm and shoulder and gently urged me upright, first to my knees, then to my feet.

"Well," murmured Sister Bernadette. Her gaze met mine from behind her wire-framed glasses, shock and sadness there in equal parts.

"*Tabarnak*," responded Sister Colette from my other side. She shoved her walker toward me in an unspoken invitation to avail myself of its built-in seat.

Despite my distinct wobble, I shook my head. Trying to stay upright was actually helping right now. It gave me something to focus on other than Drummond's words. His decree. His—

"Sister?" came a small voice from behind me.

Phoenix. I'd forgotten about her. *Fuck.* She'd have heard Drummond's message. She would know …

I closed my eyes, wishing for an instant that I could disappear the way the Mage had. That I didn't have to deal with this. That I didn't have to find words of comfort and hope inside myself that I didn't feel, or—

But instead of asking me for comfort, Phoenix instead wrapped slim arms around my waist from behind and hugged me fiercely.

"It's okay," she whispered into my ear. "Talia is strong, remember? She's got this, and she knows we'll come for her."

I couldn't speak past the lump in my throat. Talia *was* strong, it was true. But there had been all that blood on the floor when we came home that night, and she'd already suffered a concussion when Sister Margaret had whacked her over the head, and I somehow doubted that seeking medical care for her would have been high on the Mages' list of priorities.

One body part a day. I shuddered at the cruelty behind the very idea. If I lived a thousand lifetimes, I would never understand how humanity could contain so much evil at one end of its spectrum and so much good at the other. Because *how*?

Bereft of reassuring words, I lifted my hand to pat Phoenix's arm, then stopped when I saw my blackened fingers and palms. Sweet Mary Magdalene, the burns were deeper than I'd realized. They went all the way to the bone on the index and middle fingers of my right hand, and pale white gleamed beneath a fine web woven across the injury, where the stone had bound scorched skin to scorched skin.

Sister Simonne let out a little hiss as she took my hand in her own. "Do you need to see a doctor?" she asked, turning it gently this way and that as she examined the extent of the damage.

I shook my head.

She hesitated. "You're certain."

"I'm certain," I said. Medical attention would have been a given for anyone other than me with burns of this degree, but the sisters knew about the stone and how it had bound itself to me. They knew that it had held me together—quite literally—with its cobwebs after more injuries than I cared to count at this point: a shattered skull and shoulder blade in my first battle with the Mage that had come to the Mary Magdalene House for Women; a snapped ankle when I'd jumped down into the trench at the Citadelle last week …

There were undoubtedly others that I'd—well, that I'd missed in the heat of action, I supposed, because there'd been rather a lot of that. But none had been serious enough to stop me, or the stone's ability to glue me together, and now it was as much a part of me as I was of it. The two of us were inextricably bound together until I died.

Which made one of Drummond's demands pretty much impossible.

And the other demand?

My gaze strayed toward the stairs and the alien man-child hiding above us. The being who had brought my stone and five others already in Mage hands to Earth millennia before—and the only being who could tap into and use their full powers, which was exactly what the Mages wanted of him.

And which made the second of Drummond's demands pretty much impossible, too.

Fuck.

I hunched my shoulders in the circle of Phoenix's arms, and she released me and came around to join in Sister Simonne's examination of my burns. A little hiss of air left her, too, and worried brown eyes lifted to mine. "Are you sure the stone is enough to heal that?"

I hesitated. I wasn't, to be entirely honest. Most of my other injuries had been internal, apart from various scrapes and bruising—a hell of a lot of bruising—and so I'd never really *seen* what the stone's magick was able to do. I'd felt it, yes. I could still feel it wrapped around my ankle, in fact. But it had never been called on to heal my outside.

On the other hand, I reminded myself, my bruises had all *eventually* healed, so theoretically my skin would, too, right? And for now, the stone had sealed the worst of the burns and taken away the brunt of the pain so that I could function, and that was all that mattered.

"It's enough," I reassured Phoenix, who appeared torn between relief and skepticism.

Relief won. Or at least, the desire for it.

"Good," she said. "So how do we rescue Talia?"

Once again, my gaze met Sister Bernadette's, finding grim, stoic understanding there. Because *rescue*?

That might also be impossible.

CHAPTER 3

I FOUND METHUSELAH ON THE THIRD FLOOR OF THE monastery, where only he—and sometimes Phoenix in his company—ever went. Sister Bernadette had, blessedly, put her foot down about further discussion tonight, citing the need for the older nuns—especially Sister Colette (who had rolled her eyes at the suggestion)—to get their rest.

"It's late," she had said firmly, steering a protesting Phoenix toward the stairs, "and we're all tired. We will think better after some rest."

The young woman had looked to me for help, but I'd sided with the head of the Ursulines. "Sister Bernadette is right," I'd told Phoenix. "It's past midnight, and I've been up since five. I'm exhausted. We'll talk at breakfast, I promise."

Although I was certain even now that I still wouldn't have any idea what to say by then, because I wasn't likely to find the answers I needed—or to admit I already had them—in a handful of hours, regardless of whether I slept. But a promise was a promise, and it had been enough to satisfy my young charge, who had nodded and allowed Sister Lise to tug her up the stairs while Sister Bernadette went in search of a broom and dustpan for the ashes on the entry floor.

Sister Bernadette had refused to let me help, so I'd watched in silence as she'd cleaned up the floor. Then she'd made sure the door was locked—for all the good that had done us the last time—and we had climbed the stairs together and said goodnight outside her door on the quiet second floor. The nun had hesitated there, as if she might say something more, and despite the lateness of the hour, I'd half-hoped she would—and fully hoped that the words she spoke would be of greater wisdom than any I might have for myself.

But instead, Sister Bernadette had sighed and shaken her head, bade me sleep well, and disappeared into her room. I'd stared at the closed door for a long few seconds, my hand raised to knock and summon her back. I'd wanted to tell her that I wouldn't sleep well—that I wouldn't sleep at all—without someone to talk to, but she, like the others, had needed her own sleep.

So I'd turned away, finding an odd comfort in knowing that, as much as I wanted someone to tell me what to do next, at least I wasn't the only one at a loss here. Or the only one who didn't want to say what had to be said.

And now I was here, instead. On the deserted third floor, in search of the alien who was at the heart of my problem—and who would likely be feeling as lost as I was at the moment. Perhaps more so, depending on where his mind was right now.

My slippered footsteps echoed softly along the hallway as I walked. With its bare wooden floor and equally bare, wood-paneled walls, there was nothing here to absorb the sound of my passing. Even my breathing was loud in my ears.

The nuns had long since abandoned the space, and all that remained was a motley collection of furnishings left over from a bygone era. Methuselah, I knew, favored one of the rooms in particular: the third on the left. I didn't know what its original use had been—a prayer room, perhaps, given the peaceful energy that seemed to linger in it—but now it held only a small, rickety wooden footstool set before a cold fireplace, with a single, hard wooden rocking chair beside it.

The alien man-slash-child sat motionless in the latter.

In silence, I pulled the footstool closer to him and settled myself on it. It wasn't my first time perching on it, but I still breathed a tiny sigh of relief when it didn't give way beneath my weight.

I reached out and rested a hand on Methuselah's knee,

noting its boniness beneath charcoal gray pants that fit him far too loosely—as if his body was vanishing along with his mind.

"Are you okay?" I asked.

Gentle fingers turned my hand over so that the burns faced the faint light coming from a single wall sconce beside the stone chimney. There was a matching sconce on the other side, but it was missing its bulb, and I never remembered to bring one up with me, probably because every time I came up in search of Methuselah—or Phoenix—I had other things on my mind. For what it was worth, I made another mental note to do so the next time.

If there was a next time, because—

Well. Because of a lot of things I'd been thinking about for a lot of days now but wasn't yet ready to put into words. Or action.

The ancient being in the rocking chair lifted his gaze to mine. It was Methuselah the man's gaze, filled with concern but not surprise.

"I should be asking you that, don't you think?" he said.

I shrugged. "I'll heal."

It sounded more dismissive than I'd intended, but Methuselah was unfazed. He understood the stone's entanglement with me better than the others. Better, even, than I did. He turned my hand over again and gave it a pat, then withdrew a tiny plastic dragon from his cardigan pocket.

My heart sank. Was the child already here? Damn. I'd hoped for more time with the grownup; perhaps even with the ancient being behind both. But the old man in the chair only toyed idly with the figurine—fidgeted, really. He didn't run it over the hills and valleys of his legs or make roaring noises or pretend that it could fly. I cleared my throat.

"You were right," I said. "About someone coming, I mean. The consortium—the Mages—sent us a message."

Pale blue eyes flicked up to meet mine, then shifted away again. I sighed and corrected myself.

"Me. They sent me a message."

"They have your friend."

"They do."

"And they want me in return."

"They do," I agreed again. "Along with the stone."

"They'll never stop, will they?" he said, his voice heavy with—what? Sadness? Weariness? Perhaps a bit of both.

I could empathize, and I'd only been running from them for a few weeks, not hiding from them for thousands of years.

"No," I said. "No, I don't think they will."

"They can't, I suppose," he mused. "Not any more than the darkness can."

I frowned. "I don't understand."

"The darkness on which the stones feed," he said. "You know it's alive, don't you?"

Air wheezed from me, and the footstool under my butt wobbled precariously. I recovered my balance and stared at Methuselah. "It's what, now?"

"Alive," he said. "How else could it evade the stones?"

Alive. Evade.

The words on their own made sense, but as they related to the stone in my pocket? The one that had bound itself to me by devouring—by eating—by me feeding it my own dark—

That darkness?

I blinked at the ancient being regarding me quizzically. Then I blinked again. Then I blinked a third time. Then, for good measure, I flapped my mouth, too. But I still couldn't find words to articulate any of the new jumble of questions that had formed in my brain. Or the squidgy-ness slithering through me at the *alive* idea. Because getting used to the idea that the stone had bound itself to the darkness in me had been one thing, but now the darkness itself was alive?

That was a whole new level of ick.

"No," I said, fighting the urge to hyperventilate. "No, it is *not* fucking alive. It can't be."

Methuselah slumped in the rocking chair, and remorse stabbed at me as the pale blue eyes turned watery. Sweet Mary Magdalene, now I was going to make an old man cry? I dug in my pockets in the vain hope that I might find a tissue—that I never actually carried, but whatever—as he wiped a sleeve across his face and heaved another sigh, this one tremulous.

"But it is," he said quietly. "It's always been alive. And the Mages won't stop because they can't. It's taken them over. It *is* them now, and only the stones can stop it."

I didn't think anything could have distracted me from the *alive* bit, but that did it. I blinked as I absorbed the words and my own surprise. "The stones?" I echoed. "The stones can stop the darkness?"

He nodded, the movement making the chair rock a little as he stared into the empty fireplace. "They can," he said. "But not here."

I gritted my teeth against a surge of impatience. I was tired, it was too late for riddles, and—

"I need to tell you a story," said a voice, and even though it was Methuselah's mouth that moved, I jerked backward on the stool, because the voice—the voice coming from it— *wasn't* his.

Or rather, it was, *and* it wasn't.

It was deeper and more resonant, and at the same time melodious in a way I'd never heard. It was as if—

I met the crystalline, pale blue eyes and caught my breath as I saw again the stars that existed within them, and the galaxies that were behind the stars. Yes. That. The voice sounded the way the eyes looked.

Infinite.

"Will you listen?" the voice asked.

My jaw was locked tight against the breathless squeak that sought to escape my throat, but I nodded agreement. The old man with the shock of white hair that stuck out in every direction set the toy dragon on the arm of the rocking chair, folded his hands across his stomach, and settled back with a long sigh.

"Once," he said quietly, "before your world or the worlds beyond, or even the worlds beyond those existed, there were others here. Your kind would have called them gods, but they just … were. *We* just were. And at first, we were all. We were everything. There were no planets or stars, no universes or their alternates—"

My jaw dropped. Wait. *Our kind? Gods? Alternates, as in alternate universes?*

I mean, I got that the sisterhood had referred to him as an alien, yes, but this? Sweet Mary Magdalene, I had questions. Methuselah was continuing, however, and I snapped my mouth shut and shoved them aside so that I could keep up with his story. Not because I'd promised I would, because I hadn't, but because I didn't dare fall behind. Didn't dare miss any of it.

Because I didn't know if the declining alien—god?—would ever be able to tell it to me again.

"There was only us," he continued, the resonant voice taking on a faraway tone, "and the Weaver who made us, and the box."

So much for abandoning my questions. My jaw dropped open again.

Weaver? I thought.

"Box?" I sputtered.

The galaxy-filled eyes regarded me, then he held out a hand, palm up, and wiggled his fingers in a *give it here* gesture. I drew back, my own hand going to the stone's pocket protectively. The galaxy eyes and Methuselah smiled sadly.

"I will not use it," he said. "I just want to show you something."

I hesitated another instant. He was so volatile these days. So unpredictable, switching between adult and child in the blink of an eye—and now this. Did I dare?

Questions, I reminded myself. Did I dare not?

I tugged the stone from its place and held it out in my palm. The old man in the chair made no move to take it.

"Look at it," he said.

My gaze dropped to the polished black rectangle with its faint, web-like lines. It looked the same as it always had. I looked back at Methuselah and his galaxies.

"What am I looking for?"

"The edges," he said, drawing a rectangle in the air with his index finger. "What do you see along the edges?"

I peered obediently at the stone's periphery, but I could see nothing in the dim light that reached me from the sconce. The stool beneath me wobbled and squeaked a protest as I pushed to my feet. I went to stand directly beneath the light, then held the stone up between thumb and forefinger, turning it this way and that but finding noth—

Hold on. Were those marks of some kind? I squinted closer, then moved the stone further away and squinted again, both without success. Damn these aging eyes of—

The light above me flared brighter, eliciting a sharp inhale from me, along with a burst of adrenaline from the fight-or-flight part of my brain that shouted *Mages!* But as quickly as the thought formed, I knew it was wrong. If Methuselah was still sitting in the rocking chair with stars in his eyes and not warning me in his highly disconcerting way that someone was coming, then there were no Mages. Not here, not on their way.

There was only him.

CHAPTER 4

With the help of the brighter light, I found what Methuselah had wanted me to see along the sides of the stone. And once I saw them, I couldn't understand how I'd missed them before.

They were a row of what looked like tiny notches cut into the edges, equidistant from one another, uniform in both size and shape. Like one side of a dovetail joint in well-crafted furniture. Gently, I ran a fingertip along them. I could feel them, too—so again, how in the name of the holy Mother herself had I not noticed them before this?

Heaven knew I'd gripped the stone enough times that its size and shape and smoothness were all but imprinted on my memory. Held it so tightly at times that it *had* been imprinted on my palm, its edges leaving raised red welts there. I wondered if the other stones—the five the Mages held—had the same markings.

I knew that they did. But for what purpose?

"There was only us," Methuselah's voice whispered in my head, *"and the box."*

Five stones with the Mages, one with me. Six stones in total.

And six sides on a box.

Sweet Mary—

No. Fuck. Just … fuck.

The light by my head dimmed, returning me to the here and now. To Methuselah and his story. I took a deep, bolstering breath, tamped down the part of me that wanted to stick her fingers in her ears and flee the room chanting *"la la la la la"* and made myself return to the stool. My hips protested as I settled back onto it, reminding me that I hadn't done any of my stretches since … well, they just hadn't seemed important in forever.

And they weren't now.

I slipped the stone back into my pocket and felt it nestle against me. "What did it hold?" I asked. "The box."

"The opposite of us. The opposite of everything," replied Methuselah sadly. "It held the darkness."

HE'D BEEN A CHILD, HE TOLD ME—OR, AT LEAST, THE equivalent of one in the creation he and his kin had occupied. He was a new creation himself, made by three of the others who delighted in the very act of what he called making …

As versus the unmaking that was the darkness in the box.

The Weaver had explicitly told him never to touch it, never to open it.

His gaze lifted to mine again, and I shivered. The galaxies were still there, but the crystalline blue that they inhabited had turned dark and murky, making them wink in and out of existence.

He was getting tired. I could see it in the deepening lines around his eyes and mouth, the sag of his shoulders, the way his hands had gone limp in his lap. I hesitated, torn between stopping now and letting him rest, and the very real fear that if I did, he would never be this cognizant again. This coherent.

We needed to press on.

"But you did," I prompted gently. "You opened it. And then what?"

For a split-second, pitch-black claimed Methuselah's eyes, as if the sky itself had winked out of existence, and my shiver turned to a shudder. Belatedly, I remembered how powerful

Sister Bernadette had said he was—on top of the unpredictable part—and that I was alone up here with him, and that none of the others knew where I was, and—

Methuselah clasped his hands together and tightened them until his knuckles whitened. His eyes cleared again.

"Then the unmaking began," he whispered. "First, it unmade the others like me, then it began to unmake what we and the Weaver had made. It spread like a virus to everything. It infected every cell, every atom of every single living and inanimate thing in every single universe. It has swallowed whole stars, entire galaxies. And it won't stop until it unmakes everything. It is incapable of stopping."

My skin was icy to my own touch as I wrapped my arms around myself and stared at him. I felt that there should be more, that there *must* be more, because *how*? How could his story possibly end like that? Until it unmakes everything? What did that even mean?

Explain, I willed him. *Tell me what unmaking is. Tell me*—

"Some of your kind call it dark energy," said the alien sitting in the rocking chair, as if he'd heard me. "Others call it dark matter. They're all right; they just don't comprehend its full magnitude—or its nature."

"Unmaking," I croaked, tightening my arms around ribs that felt as if they might fly apart, destroyed by the darkness I knew to reside in me. "What is that?"

"What it sounds like. An undoing of what is done, an unraveling of what has been woven." Methuselah waved an encompassing hand at the room around us, his chair, me. "A destroying."

"But if it unmakes everything, it will have nothing left to unmake—does it not know that? Does it not understand?"

"You ask the wrong question," he replied.

The cold of my skin seeped inward, coiling around my heart, my lungs, my core. "It doesn't care," I said.

"Because of its very nature," he agreed, his words and voice carrying the weariness of millennia, "it cannot care."

WE SAT IN SILENCE FOR SO LONG THAT I WAS AFRAID Methuselah might nod off, exhausted by the telling of his story. A dozen times, I tried to rouse myself to ask a question—Mary Magdalene knew I had enough of those—but I was exhausted, too. I was exhausted by the weight I'd carried this far, by Ronald Drummond's message and the confirmation of what I'd already known but hoped against, and now …

Now by this. By Methuselah's words that had wormed their way into my skull and were running in an unending loop through my mind.

"It is incapable of stopping," he whispered, over and over again, *"until it unmakes everything. It cannot care."*

… incapable of stopping.

… cannot care.

… incapable of—

I sat up straight on the stool, because wait. *It* was incapable of stopping, but *it* had been contained once. By the stones. By a box made of the stones. A frisson of excitement rippled over me.

"The box," I said, tripping over my words as I tried to assemble my thoughts. "Methuselah, if we can get the stones from the Mages, if we can get all of them together again—the stones, I mean, not the Mages—can you rebuild the box?"

But even before the white head began to shake, I slumped again, recognizing the flaws in my idea. And they were many—beginning with how we could even find the stones, never mind take them away from the consortium—but one flaw in particular stood out above the rest.

And it was so very obvious.

I held up a hand to forestall Methuselah's response.

"Shit," I muttered. "You would have done that already, wouldn't you? If you could."

"I would," he agreed. "Sadly, only the Weaver could have restored the box, if I could have found her, and now ..."

The excitement that had already given up hope in me turned to cold foreboding. "Now?" I asked. "What about now?"

Again, I thought I'd lost him, he was silent for so long. I assembled every ounce of patience that I could find in myself and put my hand on his knee again, schooling myself to gentleness rather than panic.

"Methuselah?" I nudged. "What about now? Why can't the Weaver fix the box now?"

"I think the dark is unmaking her, too," he said, so quietly that, despite the tomb-like silence in the room, I had to strain to hear him. "Unless we can save her."

Then, as my utter shock became a jumble of questions churning in my brain, the old man before me held up the dragon figurine and gave me his most charming smile.

"Want to play castle with me?" his child asked. "I'll be the princess, and you can be the knight coming to rescue me. But there's only two of us, so I'll have to be the dragon, too. *Rawr*."

CHAPTER 5

"Well," said Sister Bernadette, setting a steaming mug of coffee on the table before me and taking a seat opposite with a second mug. "Well."

Tell me about it, I thought, wrapping my hands around the hot mug. The heat seared my already-scorched palms, but I didn't move them, instead letting the pain become a focal point for my brain. A desperately needed anchor in a world that had turned even more unpredictable around me. Around us all.

It was just past five in the morning, and the nun and I were alone together in the kitchen. Given the lateness of the previous night—and the trauma surrounding the Mages' message—Sister Bernadette had decided to forgo lauds and let the other nuns sleep. She'd been wide awake herself, however, and had come down to get a start on breakfast for Sister Lise, who had promised Sister Colette chocolate chip pancakes.

I'd been waiting for her.

By the time I'd coaxed the child Methuselah down from the third floor and into his bedroom, I'd abandoned any thought of sleep myself. There had been no more answers from him, of course, but that hadn't stopped me from going over and over (and over) the ones he'd already given me.

Alive.

The darkness was alive, and it was unmaking the maker— the Weaver—and I was supposed to save her.

"You're sure he used that word," she murmured, frowning as she stared toward the sink, at nothing in particular that I could see. "*Out.* He said—"

"That it was his fault that the darkness got out of the box," I finished, wincing at the impatient note in my voice, because the *out* part was the least of my concerns right now. I was much more interested in getting it back *in* the box. "Yes. I'm sure."

Sister Bernadette stood and crossed to the stove, where she expertly flipped four pancakes in a large skillet, paused, and then turned with spatula still aloft. "It was Pandora's box," she said.

I shook my head, thrown by the apparent change in topic. "What?"

"He opened Pandora's box."

The parallel hadn't occurred to me, but given how many other myths had been turned upside down by Methuselah's third-floor revelations—including that of creation itself ...

"Huh," I muttered. "You're right."

"Not that it matters," she added, returning to her seat. "We just need to know how to put it back together again."

I hadn't shared that part of Methuselah's story with her yet, and there was no easy way to go about it. I tightened my grip on the mug, wincing at its burn against my tender palms, focusing in again on the pain—the only real thing about my life at the moment. Sister Bernadette tucked her chin down and peered at me over her wire-framed glasses.

"Sister Monica?" she prompted. "You did ask him how to fix the box, didn't you?"

"I did." I squeezed harder, feeling the skin split open across my palm, then the webs crawling beneath the surface to knit me together again. "The thing is ... we might not be able to. The Weaver is the only one who can fix it, and Methuselah thinks that the dark is unmaking her, too, unless ..."

"Unless?"

"Unless we can save her."

Sister Bernadette pressed a clean dish towel against my palm where the stone's webs crisscrossed between charred, bleeding bits of flesh in an attempt to hold me together.

Good luck, I mentally told them, because my surface was the least of our concerns when it felt as if my very core had unraveled, and there was little that spiderwebs could do for that. Even if they were from a powerful stone that had once contained the living darkness itself.

"Well," Sister Bernadette said again.

It was her fifth repetition of the word since I'd dropped the Weaver bombshell, and I had to bite my tongue to keep from snapping *well, what?* at her. First, because she didn't deserve to be snapped at, and second, because deep down, I empathized entirely—I was as much at a loss as she was.

Although I was leaning toward repeatedly saying *fuck,* rather than *well.*

Still, as long as she didn't ask "what now," I'd be—

"So what now?" she asked.

Fuck.

I scowled as she lifted the dish towel, but she was frowning at the continuing ooze of blood from my blackened palm and didn't notice. She applied pressure again as she muttered something under her breath in French. It gave me a moment to compose my expression and consider her question, which, I decided, was annoying because it was precisely the same as my own, and I had no answer for either of us.

Nor was I likely to come up with one when my brain felt like someone had filled it with sludge. I could hardly connect two thoughts together, and it dawned on me that I'd been in a state of semi-shock since Methuselah had related his story to me.

I'd seen him to his room, come downstairs, and then sat in the kitchen to wait for someone else to join me. Anyone else. Anyone who might make sense of it all, and who might tell me that no, the thoughts that kept slithering through my head—

the ones that left me feeling sick and sweaty every time they skirted the perimeter of my mind—*those* thoughts were wrong. Unnecessary. Impossible.

But things were sinking in, now, and sweet Mary Magdalene, if the Weaver was who—what—Methuselah said it—she—was, and it—she—was being unmade, what in the name of the Mother herself—who was apparently the Weaver—did that mean for us? For Earth and humanity and …

I rested my arm—the one attached to the hand that Sister Bernadette wasn't holding—on top of the table and laid my head on it, face down and eyes scrunched tightly shut. My brain had done a lot of glitching over the past few weeks, as I'd learned about the Obsidian Sisterhood and the alien they protected and the stones he'd brought to Earth, but this latest?

This was epic.

And it kept feeding *those* thoughts. The ones about Talia.

The cold, sick, soul-devouring inevitabil—

My downward spiral ended as Sister Bernadette released the hand she'd been holding, settled it gently on the table alongside my head, and gave my shoulder a brisk pat.

"You should rest," she said. "You can't think when you're this tired."

I scowled into the crook of my arm. Tell that to the three million thoughts careening around the inside of my skull.

"Clearly," she added. "You can't think clearly. You need time to heal and to let all of this"—she waved a vague, encompassing-the-world hand in the air—"sink in. We both do."

I shook my head, then steeled myself and lifted it from the arm it rested on. "I don't *have* time—"

"Nor do you have a plan," she reminded me.

I almost laughed at that, because plan? I hadn't had one of those for so long now that I wasn't sure I remembered what one even looked like. But Sister Bernadette had crossed her arms over her neat white blouse and gray cardigan, and her lips were a thin, tight line below a pinched nose and determined gray eyes. I hesitated.

Once, in a former lifetime, an eon ago, I had been like Sister Bernadette. Sensible, clear-headed, objective, and in charge. I had handled dozens of women in crisis when they'd come to the Mary Magdalene House, and I'd always started with the basics, just as Sister Bernadette was doing: shelter, food, sleep, safety.

As if she'd read my mind, Sister Bernadette turned and took a pancake from a platter on the counter. Ever efficient, she'd removed them from the skillet and turned off the stove when she'd gone to get the dish towel for my hand. Now, she switched the stove back on to cook the remainder of the batter she'd prepared, then held the pancake she'd retrieved out to me. My stomach churned uneasily.

The nun lifted my hand—the one without the split palm—and put the pancake into it. "It's not much," she said, "but it will hold you until you have a proper breakfast later. You can eat it on your way to bed."

An image of my bed upstairs popped into my head, bringing a wash of weariness with it, and my resistance crumbled. Nodding my head, I closed my fingers around the still-warm pancake and stood.

"Thank you," I said, and I meant it from the bottom of my shell-shocked, exhausted heart, recognizing that somehow, I had become one of the women I had once sheltered myself. Sister Bernadette and the Ursuline nuns might not be able to offer safety anymore—no one could—but they could still provide the basics, and those would let me clear my head and think again.

Shelter, food, and sleep it would be, because three out of four would have to do.

CHAPTER 6

I SLEPT A SURPRISING FOUR HOURS, ACCORDING TO THE WIND-up clock on the nightstand beside my narrow bed. Its face glowed in the wintry morning sun streaming in through the curtainless window, and its hands declared the time to be five minutes past ten.

A half-eaten chocolate chip pancake sat beside it.

My stomach growled as I eyed the latter. Then I decided against the idea. If it had tasted like cardboard on my way up the stairs four hours ago, I doubted it would taste much better when it was stale and cold.

I swung my legs out of bed to sit up. Plus, half a cold pancake wouldn't even begin to address the snarl in my belly, or to provide the energy I was going to need to come up with that plan Sister Bernadette had mentioned.

Because she'd been right. If I was going to find the Weaver that Methuselah had talked about, I was going to need a rock-solid one. Especially when I didn't have Talia along as my wing cop. Especially when—

My breath snagged in my chest, halfway between lungs and throat. *Not yet*, I told myself. *You don't have to decide yet.*

No matter how inevitable the decision was.

I pushed to my feet and stretched to one side and then the other, wincing at the snap, crackle, and clunk of vertebrae, shoulders, and hips. I hadn't stretched or done any of my regular martial arts patterns in weeks, and the lack of discipline was taking its toll. My body felt as stiff and inflexible as —well, as my mind did right now. Both were bogged down by the vicious circle of fight-or-flight reactions I'd subjected them to.

Later, I promised both parts of me. Later, I would make

time for centering and focus and intentional movement. I'd go to the third floor, to one of the other empty rooms there, where I could move freely and be alone with my thoughts, and—

Unbidden, an image of Talia rose in my mind, and the ache that had resided in the center of my chest since that night we'd found her missing exploded, threatening to consume me.

My eyes prickled, and I squeezed them shut against a blur of tears as other images followed. Rapid-fire ones, each overlapping the other, almost faster than I could track them. Almost.

Talia, her hair tightly pulled back, with notebook in hand as she stood at the foot of my bed in the hospital after the destruction of the Mary Magdalene House for Women, and again outside the destroyed internet café. Talia sitting beside Phoenix in the coffee shop, sliding a small pile of cash and the keys to her own vehicle across the table to me. Talia leaning across to throw open the passenger door of a sedan outside St. Paul's in Kingston as the monastery burned behind me. Talia tearing spider webs from me in the dark clearing after Rusk attacked me.

Talia in the cottage.

Talia on the train.

Talia injured and bleeding on the floor of the Ursuline monastery, sending me after Phoenix and Methuselah, assuring me she would be fine.

I drew a shuddering breath and squeezed my eyes closed. That was the last memory I had of her. It was already burned into my brain, and now … now it would be imprinted on my very soul.

Because inevitable.

THE STONE FELT LIKE IT WEIGHED A THOUSAND POUNDS IN MY pocket as I went downstairs to find the others. The weight of the world across my shoulders was easily a million times that.

Sister Bernadette was coming out of the living room as I descended the last few steps. She looked me up and down over the top of her glasses and pursed her lips as she observed dryly, "I see that the rest worked wonders."

"It helped," I said. "Really."

Her gaze dropped to the half-eaten chocolate chip pancake I held. "As did the food?"

"I ..."

She shook her head and held her hand out to take the pancake from me. "Never mind. Sister Lise did some stress-baking after you went to bed. The cinnamon rolls came out of the oven ten minutes ago. You go sit with the others around the fire, and I'll get you one. Hot chocolate or coffee to go with it?"

She was being bossy again, but I didn't mind. As soon as she'd said *cinnamon rolls*, the warm, yeasty smell permeating the air had registered in my brain, and my mouth had watered. I was suddenly starving. But I was also still reeling from the inescapable decision that had finally caught up with me in my room.

"Hot chocolate," I said. "Please." In part because my system had enough adrenaline running through it right now that it didn't require any additional jolt from caffeine. Mostly because every fiber of my being craved a comfort I could no longer give it.

While Sister Bernadette went to the kitchen, sisters Lise and Simonne moved their rocking chairs over to make room for me, and Sister Simonne pulled another forward between her and Phoenix. The nuns had long since rustled up extra rockers from various corners of the monastery, hauling them down the stairs with a cheerful abandon that had made me worry for their safety. That, of course, had been before I'd seen them in action with their Molotov cocktails against the multi-human-headed serpent behind Notre Dame Cathedral.

And then again at the Citadelle, when they'd rescued me from the Mages.

One of the rockers had disappeared again, quietly and without fanfare, after Sister Margaret's betrayal. Another sat to the side, empty and waiting for the police detective that the Mages had taken. For our friend.

For my friend.

Inevitable, my little voice whispered to me.

Not yet, I whispered back. *Please not yet.*

I smiled my thanks at Sister Simonne and took my place among them. Then, as the fire crackled merrily behind the glass door of the wood stove, I dutifully showed each of the nuns my healing hands, where the stone had worked much magick while I slept. The charred flesh was already sloughing off, and sisters Simonne and Lise marveled over the finely woven spiderwebs that had replaced the skin.

Sister Colette was less impressed. "You do know that's weird, don't you?" she muttered with a grimace. Then, when Sister Lise objected, she snapped, "What? I'm only telling the truth. Spiderweb skin *is* weird."

The argument over manners was on. I disengaged from it and looked sideways at Phoenix, who had huddled into her hoodie without greeting me—or, indeed, even seeming to notice my presence.

"You okay?" I asked softly. A few seconds passed before one shoulder lifted and fell in a careless shrug. The world across my shoulders weighed a little more heavily. If she was this deep into defense mode already, what would my decision do to her? She'd already been through so very much in her short life, first with her family, then on the streets, and now with me. How much would be too much before she broke?

I tried again. "Have you seen Methuselah this morning?"

Another delay, then the hooded head shook. I hesitated, then settled back in my chair. Half of me had hoped that the alien would be down here with the nuns, ready to answer our questions and give us direction. Half of me was relieved that he wasn't, because I wasn't sure I was ready for his answers. I debated going in search of him, but of whom? Man, child, or all-seeing alien?

I didn't know what he would be, or what I *wanted* him to be.

Before I could make up my mind—about either looking for him or what I wanted to find—Sister Bernadette came into the room with a tray. Sister Colette passed me the little collapsible table she'd been using for her own mug, Sister Lise insisted on placing everything for me so that it would be within easy reach, and in seconds, I found myself in possession of a steaming mug of thick, rich cocoa and a soft, fluffy cinnamon roll still warm from the oven.

Both looked delicious. Both lost much of their taste in the face of Phoenix's silence and my own angst. Especially my angst.

Sister Bernadette expertly drew everyone's attention away from me while I ate, ensuring a continuous stream of small talk that didn't include me. The exclusion was both a blessing and a curse, though, because it left way too much room for my own thoughts.

For anticipation.

For dread.

And the second I set my finished mug on the little table, what little reprieve I'd been granted came to a crashing halt as every eye in the room fastened on me. Except Phoenix's.

It was time.

I met Sister Bernadette's gaze on the other side of our little circle. "How much did you tell them?"

"Everything," she said. "Phoenix, too."

Well. That explained the hood. I wasn't sure that I would have told the young woman myself—not everything—but that would have been a *me* problem. Like it or not, Phoenix was as much a part of this as any of us, and the time for keeping secrets and telling half-truths had long since passed.

I nodded. "Then I guess the next question is—"

"The *only* question," growled Phoenix from the depths of her hoodie, "is when are we going to rescue Talia?"

The heart in my chest splintered into a hundred pieces, because it was time for that, too. The impossible, inevitable decision.

Steeling myself, I gripped the arms of the rocking chair, pulled back my shoulders, and turned my head to look Phoenix in the eye.

"We're not," I said.

CHAPTER 7

"Bullshit!"

Phoenix exploded from her chair before the sound of my voice had faded. Her hood fell away from her head, and she was fury topped by bright pink hair as she faced me with hands balled into fists as if she wanted to hit me.

"This is bullshit," she repeated. "Talia left her *job* for you. She came *here* for you. She was kidnapped by the Mages because of you, and you're just going to abandon her? What the fuck, sister!"

Her tirade continued as she whirled away and threw herself around the room, careening from rocking chair to window, sofa to door, wall adorned by a crucifix to bookcase that hid the nuns' supply of Molotov cocktails. Each word buried itself like a fist in my gut, until I couldn't breathe past the pain of them. There was nothing in them that I hadn't already told myself, but when the accusations came from her, when they were spoken aloud—

My fists clenched and unclenched as Phoenix's feet slammed against the floor and her rant continued.

The nuns watched her in shocked silence, and Sister Bernadette caught my eye. She arched one eyebrow in silent query—an offer to intercede—but I shook my head, and she gave an almost imperceptible nod of understanding. As hard as it was to listen, Phoenix needed to vent. Needed to say all the things that she'd been bottling up for days.

"Did you even hear what they said they'd do to her?" Phoenix threw her arms wide in emphasis as she spun on her heel. "They're going to take her apart, Sister Monica. *Piece by piece.*"

Sister Simonne took off her glasses and polished them on a corner of her cardigan. Sister Lise rocked back and forth a little faster. Sister Colette pressed together lips that quivered not in anger but—if I read the expression in her teary eyes right, and I was certain that I did—in the kind of pity that stemmed from bottomless compassion.

A tremor in Phoenix's voice said that she was winding down and beginning to feel all the other emotions that had fueled her rage. She stopped in the midst of our circle to face me at last. Her hands hung at her sides, as limp as her sagging shoulders had become.

"You can't leave her," she said, her voice cracking on the words. "I won't let you. You have to at least try to get her back. *We* have to try. I can help look for her. I can find her. On the dark web—there will be things on the dark web. I'm sure of it. The Mages have to be communicating somehow. I just need a little time—but they said a week, and it's already been a day, and if they meant it—"

"Phoenix," I began, pushing up out of my rocker and reaching for her. But my touch rekindled her fury, and she wrenched away. I let my hands drop again. Then, keeping my voice even despite the anguish swelling in my throat, I tried to explain the unexplainable.

"Even if we knew where they were keeping her—" I broke off and held up a hand to ward off the interruption I sensed forming on her lips. "Even if you found where they're holding her, there are too many of them to fight. We'd never beat them, and there is too much else at stake. Sister Bernadette told you what Methuselah—"

"Methuselah is nothing but a crazy old man!" she snapped. "He plays make-believe with a toy dragon, for fucksake. How can you believe anything he tells you? How can you let him tell you not to rescue your *friend*?"

"He didn't tell me not to rescue her," I replied, my voice as calm and even as I could make it, despite my desire to snap back at her. Her description of Methuselah came from a place of fear, I knew, and my anger wouldn't help to alleviate that.

"This is *my* decision," I told the young woman, "but—"

Her mouth opened again, and I raised my hand a second time to deflect her words. Glowering, she pressed her lips together in a tight line.

"But," I continued, "Talia would make the same decision in my shoes. Deep down, you know that. We both do."

The young woman shifted her weight and hunched her shoulders.

"She wouldn't want us to come for her," I continued, my voice breaking under my own grief. My truth. "She left her job in Toronto and came here with us, yes, but it wasn't just for us. She was in this for the thousands of women who have fought to protect us—all of us—since the beginning. She was —she *is*—in it for the sisterhood, for Methuselah, for the stones. She knows what's at stake, and like all of us, she knew the risks."

Phoenix's expression was a battleground for a dozen different emotions, none of them good. It took what felt like forever before she raised her gaze to mine—dark with desperation and a plea for a glimmer of hope—as she finally began to deflate.

"You're *sure* there's no other way?" she asked.

"I'm sorry," I said. I drew her into my arms, unresisting this time, and rested my cheek against the pink hair. Without the anger that had puffed her up, she was just my Phoenix again. Tiny. Lost. Vulnerable. And so very, very sad.

"I'm sorry," I whispered again, my voice cracking. "I wish there were, my sweet. With all my heart, I wish—"

The living room door flew open, banging into the bookcase behind it and cutting me off. As one, the Ursulines surged out of their rocking chairs at the noise—even Sister Colette— and I whirled, thrusting Phoenix behind me and shielding her with my body.

Methuselah stood in the opening, waving his toy dragon through the air as he followed its progress with his child's gaze.

"They're coming," he announced. "They're coming and now they're here."

METHUSELAH'S ANNOUNCEMENT LANDED LIKE A BOMBSHELL IN our midst. An appropriate explosion of activity followed, because not one of us had any doubt about who he meant.

It might simply be their next message, of course. Their instructions as to how, in exchange for Talia's life, I was supposed to surrender myself and Methuselah—oh, and the whole damned world, too, although they'd conveniently left that part out.

It might also be that they'd decided not to take a chance on my cooperation after all, and this was another attack. Either way, the Ursuline nuns weren't taking any chances.

The four of them raced—and in Sister Colette's case, trundled—toward the bookcase that hid the cache they'd begun restocking with Molotov cocktails over the last few days. I whirled to deliver instructions to Phoenix, but she was already in motion, too, reaching for Methuselah's arm as she passed him on her way out of the room.

"I'll take him to Sister Colette's room," she told me over her shoulder. Her anger with me—and our shared grief—had been shoved aside. We were a team again.

For now.

I nodded agreement with the plan, but Phoenix, already towing Methuselah around the corner and down the hall, didn't see. Sister Colette's room was tucked away at the back of the residence. It was the only one—including the upstairs rooms—that wasn't accessed off the main hallway facing the front door, the sole entrance into the monastery and the like-liest point of entry, if Methuselah was right.

The stone I'd pulled from my pocket sat in my clenched fist, its edges digging into my fingers and palm, and its webs snaking beneath my skin to join with the strands that already ran through my body. That always ran through my body now.

They're coming.

Methuselah's warning settled into me, tugging my steps in his direction—his and Phoenix's—but I resisted. As tempting as it was to get as far away from here as fast as we could, running wasn't the answer. Because the other words Methuselah had spoken—the ones upstairs, when he'd told me about the box—had settled into me, into my very core, and made it impossible.

His words, and my response.

"They'll never stop, will they?" he'd said.

"No," I'd replied. *"No, I don't think they will."*

The certainty had fueled a second decision that I'd made but hadn't yet shared with the others. Not the one about Talia—that one really had been inevitable—but the one about the other stones. The stones the Mages had and couldn't be allowed to keep.

Three loud raps sounded on the front door outside the living room.

I released the impulse to follow the path Phoenix and Methuselah had taken and instead headed for the front entrance. The Ursulines, Molotovs in hand, followed on my heels. All of us were prepared for battle, and the webs running through my body tautened in anticipation of the same.

Sister Bernadette's expression was grim as she looked at me, a question behind it. Were we ready? I hesitated, because no. No, we were not, but we had no choice. The Mages had come to our home. We had to face them. Sister Bernadette gave a brisk nod, as if I'd somehow conveyed the thought to her, and she and the others fanned out to either side of me, their homemade firebombs at shoulder height, ready to pitch.

With her free hand, Sister Simonne reached for the door-knob and pulled open the heavy door.

A lone woman stood at the top of the monastery's concrete steps.

Chapter 8

It was hardly the attack we'd braced for.

Long seconds ticked past as we stared at our visitor. Our shock was palpable between us; a frisson of uneasy energy passed from one to the other as we stood shoulder to shoulder.

As surprised as we were to see her, however, the woman seemed remarkably un-so in return—despite the array of Molotov cocktails at the ready. Expressionless brown eyes in a mature, carefully maintained face flicked over each of us in turn, then settled on me, steady, unblinking, assessing. A neighbor trudged past in the courtyard beyond, glancing back repeatedly until they'd passed through the arched entry to the street.

Sister Colette grunted and lowered her Molotov cocktail to rest on the top of her walker beside me. "You're not—" she began.

"Yes," I interrupted. "She is."

To the right of the open door, Sister Lise frowned at me and also lowered her firebomb. "But she's—"

I cut her off, too. "It's the middle of winter," I pointed out, "and she has no coat, no boots, and there's no car out there that could have brought her." There weren't even tire tracks to say that one had been there before. There was, however, a single black feather lying in the snow three steps below and behind her. And it was huge. At least three feet long. There was no way it had come from a bird.

"She's one of them," I said. "She's a Mage."

The woman's lipsticked mouth tilted upward at the corners in a tiny smile, and she inclined her head in a gesture I suspected was meant to be gracious but came off instead as patronizing.

How fitting.

An iciness that had nothing to do with the snow swirling into the front entry settled into my belly, and my fist tightened around the stone. My gaze probed the courtyard, looking for whatever had left the feather, because I had no doubt that the woman had arrived on the Ursulines' doorstep in the company of some kind of flying monster.

Just because I found nothing didn't mean I could relax.

"Sister Monica?" prompted Sister Bernadette, waiting for me to decide on our next move. All four of the nuns had Molotov cocktails at launch-level again. Throwing the fire-bombs would mean almost certain destruction of their home, but not one of them would hesitate if I gave the word. They knew as well as I did what was at stake here, and they would do anything to keep Methuselah safe.

We would. Because we had to.

Moving for the first time since the door had opened, the woman—the Mage—at the top of the stairs lifted her hands and extended them toward us. A subtle rustle of fabric whispered through the entry as the Ursulines shifted their weight in readiness. But there was no summoning of magick. Instead, the woman rotated her hands so that I could see the backs of them, with their manicured nails coated in neutral polish. My eyebrows twitched together for an instant, and then I understood.

Her fingers were ringless. She might be a Mage, but she wasn't with the consortium. Not comforting, exactly, but perhaps less threatening.

Infinitesimally speaking.

I tuned into the webs that bound me to the stone. The ones running through my body had relaxed again, and the stone itself had subsided into an inert warmth. Like me, it seemed to sense no threat here, at least for the moment.

But I still didn't return it to my pocket.

"Let her in," I told Sister Simonne, and then, as the

heavyset nun stepped aside, I added in a growl to the stranger, "You have five minutes, then *I* throw the first Molotov."

HER NAME WAS REBECCA MONTEREY, SHE TOLD US. HER FACE wasn't as unlined in full light as it had been in the shadows, and she took my threat seriously.

We escorted her into the living room, not to be polite, but so we could close the door and keep our conversation with her from drifting down the hall to where Phoenix and Methuselah hid in Sister Colette's room. And, more importantly, to keep her from accidentally hearing them.

We did not, however, invite her to sit.

She stood in the center of the room, and I sized her up as she began to speak. Her blond hair was as carefully maintained as her face, cut in a chin-length bob, and I put her at about fifty years old. She carried herself with the kind of assurance that came with power, which made sense, given her Mage status, and she was well but conservatively dressed in a long-sleeved, charcoal gray dress that hit just below the knee. A string of pearls rested against it, and she was still wearing the sensible, matching pumps she'd neglected to remove in the front entry.

The latter was an affront that had caused Sister Lise to scowl and open her mouth, but Sister Bernadette had touched the nun's arm and shaken her head, and Sister Lise had swallowed the objection sitting on the tip of her tongue. She'd settled for pointedly staring at Rebecca Monterey's feet while the woman laid out the reasons for her visit.

Ms. Monterey just as pointedly ignored the stare.

"The group I belong to is not affiliated with the Ascent Consortium," she informed us in a brisk voice. "We're a collective of independents who simply wish to see balance restored in the world."

One of the Ursulines snorted, whether at the way Rebecca distanced herself from the consortium while still confirming her Mage status, the very concept of Mages and balance, or both, I didn't know. It didn't matter, and I inwardly snorted at both of those, myself—not to mention at the consortium's name, because *Ascent*? Of course they'd call themselves something like that. A name that held supreme confidence, superiority, and the intent to dominate, all neatly bundled together.

"*Anyway*," our uninvited guest continued, ignoring the snort, Sister Lise's continuing glare at her still-shod feet, and my own undoubtedly skeptical expression, "we know that you, Sister Monica, have one of six stones brought to Earth by an alien, and that the consortium has the remaining five. We also know that you protect the alien, and that the consortium has taken the police detective as hostage in exchange for you turning it over to them."

"It—you mean the stone?" My obtuseness was deliberate, because if *it* referred to Methuselah, as I suspected it did, the pronoun told me worlds about the Mage and her "collective."

"The *alien*," she said, narrowing her eyes as if suspecting that I was being thick on purpose.

"*He* has a name," Sister Colette informed her sourly, apparently of the same opinion as me, "and *he* is more human than any of you lot at this point."

Rebecca's attention shifted to the nun leaning on the walker. Her gaze traveled over Sister Colette's hunched frame as she cataloged her, found her wanting, and turned her back without responding. Dark, impatient eyes met mine, and she opened her mouth to resume the explanation of her presence. Or the story. Or whatever.

I cut her off before sound emerged. "What kind of balance?" I asked.

Her lips snapped shut again, and her expression turned—

deliberately, I thought—blank as she blinked at the sudden change in subject. "Pardon?"

"What kind of balance, exactly? You said your"—I waved the fingertips of my empty hand in the air—"*collective* wanted to restore balance in the world. What kind of balance? And by whose definition?"

"I'm not sure what you mean," she hedged, the tightness around her eyes telling me I'd asked the right question.

"You know exactly what I mean," I replied. "And I'm not continuing this conversation without an answer. What is your collective's idea of balance? Is it equity? Fairness? Inclusion? Does it include a seat at the table for everyone, or just a select few?"

Rebecca Monterey's mouth tightened to match her eyes as her controlled demeanor cracked a little. "If you mean, do we believe in Utopia," she retorted, "then the answer is no. And neither do you, if you're honest."

I inclined my head. "Perhaps not," I agreed, "but neither do I believe in an elite few holding all the power. Especially not if they're Mages on top of everything else."

She visibly bristled and made a concerted effort to bring herself under control before responding a little tartly, "At least *we're* not trying to destroy the entire planet the way the consortium will if they're not stopped."

I stared at her, dumbfounded. Was she serious? And that deluded? "*That's* your argument?" I snorted. "That you should be in control instead of them, because you'll do slightly less damage?"

"Someone has to hold the reins, Ms. Barrett—"

"Sister Monica will do."

"Sister," she echoed after a pause that lasted just long enough to make it clear what she thought of my title. "It's a well-known fact that a lack of leadership only results in instability and chaos. It leaves a power vacuum that invites evil to take control."

I raised an eyebrow, giving her a moment to recognize the incongruity of her own words. The outright, complete lack of self-awareness. But nope. Her own statement went right over her head, and her expression turned earnest. Rebecca Monterey had well and truly hit her stride now.

"Think what you will of us," she continued in her effort to convince me of her sincerity, "it doesn't change the fact that we're as interested in stopping the consortium as you are—"

I'll just bet you are.

"—and we can help you get the police detective back in exchange."

The entire room went so still that I could hear the snow crystals hitting the living room window behind Sister Bernadette. I felt the gaze of every Ursuline in the room focused on me, waiting for my reaction—watching to see if I would take the stone from my pocket and strike down the Mage.

Or perhaps that last part was just me.

I curled my fingers into my burnt palms, digging the nails in hard to keep myself from doing just that. Willing my darkness to subside beneath my surface again.

"You know where she is?" I asked at last.

"We do. And we're prepared to see that she's returned to you."

"In exchange, you said. For what?"

"The other stones," Rebecca Monterey said, as calmly as if she were asking for a cup of sugar. "Not yours. Only theirs. We can help you find them, you take them and bring them to us, and we will get your friend back for you."

A horn tooted outside in the courtyard, and she cocked her head to one side. "That will be my taxi. Think about our offer. I'll be in touch."

Not one of us moved to stop her as, with the same supreme confidence she'd entered with, she walked past us and into the front hall. A second later, we heard the door open and close, and she was gone, her messaged delivered. Perhaps not with the same fanfare as Drummond's had been, but certainly with just as much impact.

"*Tabarnak*," muttered Sister Colette.

"*Câlice*," agreed Sister Simonne.

Sister Bernadette's gaze swept over them and landed on me. "Fuck," she said.

CHAPTER 9

We didn't immediately discuss Rebecca Monterey's offer. Mostly because I couldn't.

There were too many conflicting thoughts whirling through my brain, all vying for my attention—half of which was centered on the spiderwebs crawling through me and wrapping around my heart and lungs and slithering through my skull.

I knew what they were looking for, of course, because the other half of my attention was on that. The darkness—alive, if Methuselah was to be believed—that had somehow grown exponentially in the wake of Mage's visit. A darkness that whispered things to me that I knew better than to listen to but still heard. Tempting things. Things like promises of revenge and release.

And sweet Mary Magdalene, that last one …

The clink of a spoon against a stoneware bowl startled me back to the dining room table and the silent midday meal. Silent referring to a lack of discussion rather than a dearth of sounds, because there were plenty of those, each louder than it needed to be, each like fingernails on the chalkboard of my nerves.

Sister Simonne's habit of sniffling after she swallowed each bite of food, the way Sister Bernadette kept shushing Sister Colette every time the latter cleared her throat and scowled in my direction …

Another clink of spoon against bowl became the last straw. I pushed back from the table and stood. Four pairs of eyes fastened on me, and four spoons stopped halfway to their diners' mouths.

"I need—" I stopped, digging my fingers into the napkin I

clutched in both hands and biting back the *"everyone to shut up"* that sat on my tongue. Too harsh, I told myself.

"Quiet," said Sister Bernadette, "and time to think."

I nodded, blinking back a sudden rush of tears at her calm understanding. If she knew, if she even guessed at the turmoil inside me ...

"Go," she said. "We'll call you for dinner, and we can talk then."

I went, carried out on a wave of compassion and concern that followed me up the stairs and down the hall to my room. Blessedly, I didn't meet either Phoenix or Methuselah on the way. Both had been absent from the table, Methuselah because he rarely joined us in the first place, and Phoenix because—

Well. I hadn't been there when Sister Lise had filled her in on Rebecca Monterey's visit, but I could just imagine what a twist she'd be in at the moment. A twist I wouldn't be able to deal with right now. Not before I'd sorted through my own.

Because holy Mother of All, what a twist.

I stopped in front of my bedroom door and, hand on the knob, leaned my forehead against the cool of the dark-stained wood and closed my eyes. A shudder rippled through me, starting in my core and working its way down my spine and along my limbs.

My decision regarding Drummond's demands had been crystal clear. Absolute. Inescapable. Whatever happened, whatever the consortium did, I could not, would not, give Methuselah or my own stone to them. I was certain that it was what Talia would want. We had all agreed on it, even, reluctantly, Phoenix. All that had remained was to tell the nuns about the other part of my decision, because just as I could not let my own stone fall into their hands, I could not let them keep the ones they already had, either. Somehow, I had to find a way to take them from them.

And then Rebecca Monterey had arrived and taken an

already-impossible situation, turned it on its head, and put it through a blender, leaving me with options that ranged from my original bad to worse to a brand-new level of madness.

Because now I had a way not just to find the stones but to do what we'd all thought impossible. I could save Talia, too. Or at least most of her. All it would take was an alliance with Mages.

The very idea wasn't just insane, it was *fucking* insane, but the alternative—leaving Talia to be taken apart piece by piece by the consortium, when I might be able to prevent it—was equally so.

The stone's webs stirred along my veins and wound a little tighter into the sinews of my muscles. And then there was that. The push and pull of the dark and that which wanted to contain the dark. Whispered promises of revenge that were as seductive as they were ugly. The rise of the spiderwebs threading through me not just when I needed them but all the time now, as if they were devouring me along with the dark.

My gaze strayed to the back of the hand resting on the doorknob, and the words etched on the skin there, faded now by age and marred by wrinkles. NO REGRETS, the words said. They'd held great meaning for me when I'd had the tattoo done after leaving the convent and starting the Mary Magdalene House for Women, but now ... now, it felt like they taunted me, because no regrets? In the midst of all this? Who the fuck was I kidding?

Gritting my teeth, I tried to dial back my emotions. Anger made it worse, I reminded myself, twisting the doorknob. Anger, impatience—the dark took any negative impulse as an invitation, and the stone was increasingly quick to respond.

I pushed into the room.

If I was going to see any of this through, if I was to stand a chance, I needed to find a way to focus. To stay calm. To—

I stopped short as someone in the chair by the window turned their head toward me.

A hoodie-wearing someone.

The thought—and all the good intentions behind it—dropped away, and my shoulders climbed back up to my ears. I loved Phoenix with all my heart, but right now?

Right now, fuck.

Just fuck.

MY HAND TIGHTENED ON THE DOORKNOB. A CONFRONTATION with the young woman didn't even remotely fit with the time and space I needed to sort through Rebecca Monterey's proposal—or the decision I needed to make—and for a moment, I was seriously tempted to just turn around and leave again, comfortable clothes be damned.

But I didn't. Instead, I closed the door behind me and leaned against it.

"So, this is where you got to," I said. "If I'd known, I would have brought you some lunch. Sister Lise made beef barley soup." At least, that's what I thought it had been, although it could have been anything, for all the taste it had held in the few bites I'd had.

"Thank you, but I'm not hungry." Phoenix was curled into a ball on the chair, her feet tucked up onto the seat in front of her and the body of her hooded sweatshirt tugged over her knees. She'd pulled her hands inside the sleeves, and she appeared a fraction of her normal size, which, I suspected, was how she felt right now. And noting how the bones of her shoulders stood out beneath the fabric, I thought it might actually be true, too. I frowned.

"You need to eat, Phoenix."

She rolled her eyes.

"I'm worried about you," I said. "You're not—"

"Myself?" she interrupted on a bitter note, wrapping arms around her knees in a hug. "Are any of us ourselves anymore?"

The question held more truth for me than for any of the others, in a very literal sense, but she didn't need to know that right now.

"Maybe not," I admitted. Standing away from the door, I crossed the room to my bed and sat down on the edge nearest her, then rested my elbows on my knees and linked my fingers together. "What's going on?"

"Do you trust her?" she asked. "That Monterey woman?"

I didn't need to think about my answer. Not when a dissonance still permeated the monastery long after Rebecca Monterey had departed. An imbalance. Like remnants of a darkness that far, far surpassed my own.

"No," I told Phoenix. "No, I don't trust her."

"But you'll still do it. You'll still let her help."

I wasn't sure if it was meant as a statement or a question. Not that it mattered, because my answer would have been the same either way.

"I don't know," I admitted. "I haven't decided. There's a lot at stake. A lot besides Talia, I mean."

She inhaled a sharp breath and turned her face to the frost-patterned window. A single tear tracked down her cheek.

"She wouldn't want us to," she said finally. "She wouldn't want *you* to take the risk. She'd be the first to tell us not to trust that woman or her collective."

Except, for all the reasons I'd been going over and over— and over—in my mind, it wasn't that simple.

"They'll never stop, will they?" Methuselah's voice whispered in my memory, along with my reply.

"No. No, I don't think they will."

To say that I was torn would have been like saying that a Quebec winter was cold, because Phoenix was right about Talia. The Toronto police detective who'd had my back through multiple Mage encounters would absolutely *not* want me to even contemplate joining forces with one of their factions. On the other hand, she wasn't here to stop me, and a tiny germ of an idea had taken root in my brain and begun to unfurl into the start of a plan. Probably not a good plan, but a plan nonethe—

"I've been looking for her, you know."

I blinked at Phoenix. "Pardon?"

"Talia. I've been looking for her. On the dark web."

This time, I blinked and wheezed, my germ of a plan forgotten. "Are you sure that's wise? Have you forgotten what happened at the internet café in Toronto?"

Phoenix waved an impatient sleeve at me. "Of course I haven't forgotten, but I didn't know then that the Mages were tracking me, remember? I'm being a *lot* more careful this time. Sister Bernadette's system isn't much, so all I'm really doing is scanning for mentions or conversations involving Drummond, anyway."

She paused, then added thoughtfully, "Although, if I can find out who the other consortium members are, I suppose I might be able to hack into someone's system, too. Maybe get their personal emails."

I wheezed again, and she rolled her eyes at me.

"You worry too much," she said, with the invincible confidence of youth. "I'm hiding my location, and I'll start small until I'm sure I can get in and out without being noticed. I just … I just can't sit around doing nothing, you know?"

I had so many objections to what she was doing that I didn't even know where to start. But I also saw her point. And if it kept her occupied and feeling like she was contributing, that wasn't a bad thing. I shifted my weight on the bed and straightened my back to ease the ache in my shoulder— perhaps genuine and perhaps psychosomatic, tied into my memories of Toronto that included far more than just the internet café.

"You'll be *very* careful?" I asked.

"I'll be *very* careful," she promised, uncoiling herself from the chair and standing with the ease of someone who wasn't being held together by spiderwebs and magick. "And now I think I'll go have some of that soup after all. Beef barley, you said?"

I nodded, but she was at the door, waving cheerfully over her shoulder at me as she vanished into the corridor, leaving me to stare after her.

CHAPTER 10

We heard from Rebecca Monterey the next morning via the delivery of an expensive arrangement of nuts, dried fruit, and chocolate accompanied by a plain white envelope containing a hotel business card. On the back of the card, written in perfect cursive, were the name of a restaurant and a time—*Bistro Alexandre, 11:30*—along with a single initial.

R.

I read the summons—because that's what it was, fancy cellophane-wrapped tray or no—aloud to the others as we stood in the front entry. A scowling Sister Simonne relieved me of the tray as soon as I finished.

"I know it's wasteful," she said, lifting her multiple chins and looking at each of us in challenge, "but no. Just no. I don't trust that woman as far as I can throw her. Who knows what she's put in here?"

Sister Colette grunted and moved her walker to one side. "You'll get no argument from me," she said, waving a wrinkled hand in the direction of the kitchen.

Carrying the platter as if half-expecting it to explode if she moved the wrong way, Sister Simonne marched down the corridor. By unspoken mutual agreement, the rest of us waited, and a second later, we heard a thud, followed by the clang of the garbage can lid being decisively returned to its place. A collective sigh of relief went up. Sister Simonne hadn't been the only one half-expecting an explosion.

Sister Bernadette lifted her hands and pushed back the sleeve from her left wrist and tutted. "It's past eleven already. She certainly left it late enough, didn't she?" she muttered. She let her sleeve fall back into place and peered at me over her glasses. "You're sure about doing this?"

"I'm sure," I said. Or lied.

Whatever, because it didn't matter. I was doing it anyway.

I handed the business card to her and reached for my coat. I'd walked the streets of the old city enough times to know where the hotel was, to recognize the name *Bistro Alexandre* as its restaurant, and to know that it would take me a good fifteen minutes to walk there. Twenty, if the sidewalks hadn't been cleared after last night's snow.

Sister Bernadette had gone silent, and I paused to glance over my shoulder at her. And at the others. And the varying degrees of disapproval written across their faces. I sighed and let the hand holding my coat drop to my side.

"We talked about this last night," I said, reminding them of our extensive discussion around the fire while our hot chocolate had gone cold. "We've heard nothing more from Drummond or his consortium, and today is day three of the week he said they'd give me. I think they're hoping the wait will make me desperate. Impulsive. It's a game to them, and I can't win if I let them keep making all the rules. You know that."

The nuns exchanged glances, and Sister Colette rattled her walker in irritation.

"You can't win this way, either," she said bluntly. "*You* know that."

She was referring to Talia, of course, and I had to wait a moment for the webs around my lungs to let me breathe again. Despite all the centering and focusing and mindful movement that I'd done yesterday after talking to Phoenix, I hadn't been able to entirely undo them. I had, however, come to terms with their presence.

Ish.

And to find an odd kind of peace in that.

I met Sister Colette's irritated concern with some of that peace now. "I do know," I said. "Just as you know there is no way that I *can* win that particular battle, sister. This … alliance

... with Rebecca Monterey is a gamble, yes. But if he"—I nodded toward the stairs, where Methuselah sat beside Phoenix, *rawring* softly to himself as he slid his dragon down the banister—"is to be believed about the darkness and the Weaver, then it's a gamble we have to take."

Sister Colette opened her mouth as if to argue, but snapped it shut again when Sister Bernadette put a hand on her shoulder. Sister Lise bustled forward and took my coat from me, helping me into it and then doing up the buttons for me, deeming my hands still too badly burned for me to manage.

They were not, because the stone's magick had woven a fine, gauze-like layer of webs over both my palms that was tougher by far than my own skin, and I felt none of the pain I might have otherwise endured. But I was too preoccupied with my upcoming encounter with Rebecca Monterey to argue with the nun. Besides, it made Sister Lise feel good to help, just as it made Sister Simonne—returned from her tray-dumping mission—feel good to stand by with the rest of my winter garments in hand, ready to pass them to Sister Lise as needed.

I met Sister Bernadette's gaze over Sister Lise's head. "I'll be fine," I told her, then glanced around the hall, encompassing the others in my reassurance, too—especially Phoenix.

"It's a public place," I added, "and the Christmas market is in full swing. There will be a ton of people at the hotel. If she'd wanted to harm me, it would have been smarter to try here, where it's quiet. And the operative word there is *try*, because ..." I trailed off and shrugged, and Sister Lise tutted as the movement tugged one of the coat buttons away from her fingers.

"Well," I said, leaving the thought unfinished and knowing that all present would be able to fill in the blanks. Because a single Mage against me and the stone? It would not go well for the Mage. I was far more concerned about leaving the monastery unprotected.

I looked across at Phoenix again. "You'll stay here? With …?" I nodded at the old man sitting beside her, seemingly oblivious to the undercurrents of tension.

"Of course."

Sister Lise took my scarf from Sister Simonne and wrapped it three times around my neck, covering half my face. My toque was next, followed by a pair of thick, woolen gloves. She held up one of the latter, and I held up a fist in response, the stone clenched tightly in it.

I stretched my neck up to free my nose and mouth from the scarf's confines. "Mittens might be better," I said. Because there was no way in hell the stone was going back into its usual pocket when I was on my way out the door to meet a Mage.

Sister Colette heaved a sigh. "Use mine," she muttered. "If you insist on doing this, at least do it warm."

Sister Lise handed the gloves back to Sister Simonne in exchange for a pair of mittens. Bright purple and two sizes too big for Sister Colette's tiny hands, they'd been gifted by a neighbor who was of the opinion that the nuns needed some color in their lives. Three of the four had eschewed them— members of the highly feminist Obsidian Sisterhood or not, the training and habits of their monastic community ran deep —but Sister Colette had seized on them, declaring herself old enough not to care about conventions anymore.

Sister Lise slipped the mittens over my hands, made a final adjustment to the scarf, and stepped back with a satisfied nod. "*Bon*," she said. Good. "You are ready."

As ready as I could be, anyway.

"I could come with you and sit at another table," Sister Bernadette offered, her brow knit into a little knot above worried eyes. "Just in case."

"And do what, throw your coffee at them if there's an

attack?" Sister Colette snorted. "Leave the woman alone. Whether we like it or not, she knows what she's doing."

Sister Bernadette's lips tightened. I didn't blame her, because "the woman" most assuredly did *not* know what she was doing and had been second- and third- and fourth-guessing herself ever since she'd decided to accept Rebecca Monterey's offer, but sure. We'd go with Sister Colette's theory.

I stepped across the narrow hallway to stand in front of Sister Bernadette, lifting one of her hands in the mittened one of mine that didn't have a death grip on the stone. "Thank you for the offer," I said, "but it's best if all of you stay here, because ... well, because."

Because while I was pretty sure that Rebecca Monterey's collective was a real thing that did oppose the consortium, a dozen other scenarios were possible, too. Including but not limited to the ones that the Ursulines had floated when I'd told them yesterday that I intended to accept the alliance.

Talia, Sister Colette had pointed out rather brutally, might already be dead.

The consortium, Sister Lise had added, could be watching the monastery, waiting for me to leave so that they could take Methuselah—and likely Phoenix, too.

So could Rebecca Monterey's collective, Sister Simonne had said—or *I* might be the target for both groups.

We might still have been sitting around the fire arguing if it hadn't been for Methuselah skipping into the room and dropping down to sit at Phoenix's feet, his face turned up hopefully, and his ever-present dragon toy clutched in one hand.

"Can you tell me the princess story again?" he'd asked her. "The one where the dragon saves her from the mean prince? I like dragons."

Our argument and the evening had ended there, word-lessly resolved by the presence of the man-child-alien—a reminder of what was really at stake. The reminder that there were no right answers and no certain paths, and that, no matter what I did—what *we* did—there would be no perfect outcome.

I could see the remembrance of that in Sister Bernadette's expression and the way her gaze traveled briefly to Methuselah on the stairs.

"Because," she agreed.

She reached up with the hand I wasn't clutching and patted a tiny spot on my cheek left uncovered by the scarf. "May the Mother of All be with you," she said. "Be careful."

CHAPTER 11

Rebecca Monterey's hotel wasn't far from the monastery, but I was still half frozen and supremely grateful for Sister Lise's triple-wrapping of the scarf around my face when I arrived there. A harsh, bitter wind coming in from the St. Lawrence River snaked through the streets, driving the previous night's snowfall before it and whipping it into the faces of pedestrians.

First-time tourists were easily identifiable by their lack of adequate clothing, hunched shoulders, and grim expressions as they tiptoed their way across icy sidewalks. Residents equally so by their staid nonchalance, scrolling their phones in one gloved hand and carrying coffee-to-go cups in the other as they dodged the tourists.

I paused outside the hotel doors for a moment to gather myself and sink into my resolve. Like it or not, I needed Rebecca Monterey's help, and I needed to be sure that she believed I would help her in return. That was the only way this would work. The only chance I might have to save Talia. The only way to get the stones away from Drummond.

I could do this.

I had to do this.

I pushed through the brass-framed glass doors into the vestibule, then through a second set of doors into the sleek, ultra-modern hotel lobby that was entirely out of keeping with the old-world feel of the cobblestone streets and stone buildings outside. Pulling the mittens from my hands, I tucked them into my pocket, then unwrapped the face-saving scarf. Then, blinking the icicles from my eyelashes, I looked around me, found the restaurant Rebecca Monterey had named, and steeled myself.

Time to beard the Mage in her den.

So to speak.

THE HOSTESS AT THE ENTRANCE TO BISTRO ALEXANDRE looked me up and down as I approached, her expression screaming skepticism at my ability to afford to eat there. I couldn't read most of what was listed as the lunch *table d'hôte* on the board behind her, but if the discreet "45" written at the bottom referred to its cost, she was right. I preempted her objection.

"I'm meeting someone," I said, pointing to where I'd already spotted Rebecca. Following the direction of my gaze, the hostess looked even more doubtful, but the Mage who had been watching for me from a corner booth on the far side of the restaurant raised a hand in acknowledgment, and the young woman stepped back to let me pass. Leaving drips of melting snow in my wake, I threaded my way between the tables.

Rebecca was watching the street outside the window with an air of boredom as she waited for me, tapping her polished nails against the tabletop covered in a crisp white cloth. I slid into the banquette seat opposite her, coat and toque still in place and scarf hanging from my neck, and shook my head at the server approaching with a pot of coffee. I didn't plan to be here long.

"Are you sure?" Rebecca asked in her measured, cultured tone. "It's my treat."

"Then definitely not," I said. Annoyance flashed across her expression, quickly masked by studied poise. I didn't care. Nor did I waste time. "You said you know where Talia is."

She inclined her head. "We do."

"And that you can get her out."

"We can."

"Safely?"

"My word is my bond, Sister Monica. We can make no guarantees, of course, but we will do our best."

"Then I'll do it. I'll get the stones."

The perfectly colored lips curved into a shape reminiscent of a fishhook. The pseudo smile did not reach the Mage's eyes. "Excellent," she said. "The others will be pleased that we have reached an agreement."

My *others* were already markedly less so, although Rebecca's assurance that we would—might—actually get Talia back would—might—alleviate some of the angst.

Some.

Maybe.

"I have a question, though." I had many, but we'd start with the most obvious.

"Of course."

"Why haven't you gone after the stones yourselves?"

A shadow crossed her face. "You saw what happened at the Citadelle. Drummond kept the stones in his condo at the top of his tower in New York City, which is even more of a fortress, magickally speaking. It's heavily warded, and there are multiple monsters a ley line away—can you imagine the devastation if we'd attempted an attack there?"

I tried to sort through what amounted to another boatload of information contained in her few words. The more I talked to this woman, the less I knew. And a Mage with a conscience, who cared what might have happened to innocent bystanders? I had *not* expected that.

Nor had I expected fantastical concepts such as a magickal fortress, wards, or ley lines, but as much as I wanted to explore them—and ask a *lot* more questions—the majority of my brain was stuck on the more immediate problem of the New York City part of Rebecca's reply. Because seriously? I supposed it would be better than somewhere overseas or in the bowels of a volcano, but not by a lot. There was still an international border that had to be crossed—and without a passport, yes, that would be comparable to descending into a volcano.

"Although we might as well have done so, given what happened anyway," Rebecca continued, and I gave my head a little shake, trying to catch up with her words.

After *what* had—

The proverbial light bulb illuminated. She'd said Drummond kept the stones in his condo at the top of his tower— past tense. That had to have meant the iconic Drummond Tower itself, infamous for its sheer, ostentatious lavishness. And if that was the case—

I frowned. "Wasn't there an explosion or something there in the fall?"

I vaguely remembered headlines to that effect in one of the newspapers that Talia used to have delivered with our groceries to the cottage in Kingston. She liked to stay in the loop, she said, even if that loop was drawing tight around the world's throat.

Talia.

I turned away from the memory. Across the table, Rebecca's mouth had drawn thin.

"Or something," she agreed. "Drummond was helping a god open a portal to one of the other slivers when the Crones interfered—specifically, the Fifth Crone. Their battle took out the entire building and half the city block."

My jaw had dropped. Confusion and disbelief battled for supremacy in deciding what question to ask first, and it took me several seconds to form one that was even remotely coherent.

"Portal-god-Crone?" I choked out, and one of Rebecca's meticulously plucked and penciled-in brows arched upward.

Okay, that maybe hadn't been as coherent as I'd intended. I tried again.

"Slivers?" I squeaked.

The immaculately maintained brows twitched together. "The sisterhood doesn't know about the slivers?"

They hadn't mentioned gods, either. At least, not plural ones. Or portals. Or Crones.

"I don't—I'm not sure—maybe once—" I stopped as I remembered the fire that had wiped out the Obsidian Sisterhood's archive and taken the life of the woman who had been painstakingly building it. Between that and the fact that none of the Obsidian sisters I'd encountered had mentioned *slivers*, I suspected that whatever might have been known about them was long gone.

I shook my head. "No. I don't think so. Their record-keeping was deliberately sparse, and whatever stories they did write down were destroyed."

A brief admiration glinted in her eyes. "What they didn't know couldn't be taken from them," she murmured. "Smart."

Yes. Right up until what none of them knew became critical *to* know. But that was history that I couldn't change now. I would have to get whatever information I needed from Rebecca. I gestured to a server a couple of tables away, and when he arrived, ordered a coffee. Then, as he turned away, I stopped him.

"Wait," I said. "Make that a maple latte, please. And I'll have the lunch special, too. She's paying." I jabbed a finger toward Rebecca.

The Mage arched an eyebrow again, but she didn't demur, and the server nodded and continued on his way to the kitchen. I shrugged out of my coat, slipped my scarf from around my neck, plucked the toque from my head, and let all the garments drop to the banquette seat beside me.

Then I rested my elbows on the table, arms folded before me, and said, "Educate me. What the hell are slivers?"

CHAPTER 12

A multiverse. The slivers were a multiverse. Because of course they were.

And they had been created by the Crones, witches who were empowered by yet another of those plural gods Rebecca had mentioned—in this case, one who called herself the Morrigan—because of course they were. And—

And sweet Mary—

No.

Fucking hell fit better here. Fucking, fucking hell.

I stared down at the cold shrimp pasta on my plate. With its congealed sauce, it didn't look nearly as fancy now as it had when the server had brought it. Ditto for the bowl of creamy bisque sitting beside it that was supposed to have been the meal's starter. I returned to my random, sputtering attempts to piece together what Rebecca had told me.

Little splinters of Earth, sliced off by Crone magick whenever a god named Morok got too powerful, trapping a part of his powers in each of them. There had been dozens of them over the millennia, the last one happening on the day of John F. Kennedy's assassination. Something about that tugged at a corner of my mind, but when I tried to bring it to the forefront, it slipped away again.

I went back to the magickal multiverse idea. How had the Obsidian Sisterhood not known about it? Would it have mattered if they had? I couldn't see how. Their protection of Methuselah and the stones would have remained the same, and—

The something tugged again. And again, it vanished when I reached for it.

Hell.

Fucking hell.

I rested an elbow on the table beside my untouched plate and rubbed my fingers over my forehead as I stared at the Mage on the other side. A new thought popped into my head, something that Sister Margaret had said in the fast-food restaurant in Kingston, when she'd told me about the alien named Methuselah and the six stones he'd brought to Earth. When she'd told me about the Obsidian Sisterhood and their connection to—

"Midwitches," I said.

Not nearly as affected by our conversation as I was, Rebecca finished chewing the last bite of her own pasta dish, swallowed, and dabbed at her lips with a pristine white napkin. She set the napkin aside. "What about them?"

I hesitated, weighing the wisdom of sharing any kind of Obsidian Sisterhood details with a Mage. But again, I was pretty sure that ship had sailed. If I was going to pull this off, I needed all the information I could get. Information the sisterhood no longer had—or maybe never had—and Rebecca might. I lowered my hand from my forehead and tucked it beneath the table with the other that still clutched the stone.

"Sister Marg—one of the sisterhood told me that the midwitches were ..." I trailed off, because Margaret hadn't really defined their role, now that I thought about it. She'd only said that they were the magickal equivalent of Mages, but on the side of the sisterhood. I started again. "She said that the Obsidian sisters were—are—witches like the midwitches, but that we don't practice magick."

"Don't you?" Rebecca pointedly dropped her gaze to the table under which my fingers traced the outline of the stone in my other palm.

"That's—" I broke off as yet another idea surfaced. I was just full of those today, wasn't I? But this one made me catch my breath. I'd been about to say that the stone was bound to me because of its own powers, because it fed off my darkness, but another snippet of my conversation with Margaret had come back to me. The one where she'd said that I, too, was a witch, and that the stone had bonded to me because of the magick I hadn't known I possessed.

I'd been more than happy to let go of that possibility when we got to Quebec City and Sister Bernadette told me about the darkness aspect. Somehow, thinking of myself as filled with darkness had seemed more acceptable than believing in witchcraft ... and sweet Mary Magdalene, if that wasn't a lesson hammered into my psyche over a lifetime by my father and the church, I didn't know what was.

But that was a revelation to take out and examine another time. Right now ...

"My magick," I murmured. "Is that what's keeping the stone from destroying me like it did the others? Except— weren't they magick, too? The Mages that it—?"

"They were. But you're ... different. You're ..." She broke off, wrinkling her nose slightly as if she'd had a whiff of something unpleasant. "Innately good, I suppose one might say."

I almost choked, biting back a guffaw. Me? Innately good? Had she *seen* what I'd done to get here? What I'd done to the Mages in Toronto and on the train in my efforts to protect first the women of the Mary Magdalene House, and then Phoenix and Talia and the stone, and now Methuselah and—

The very center of my center paused and went still.

Protection, I thought. I'd been trying to protect them. Trying to protect the innocent, the way I'd done my entire life. My life of service to others.

Innate good, my center whispered back.

"Well, hell," I muttered.

OUR SERVER RETURNED, INTERRUPTING MY SPIRALING thoughts. I waited while he cleared our table, reassuring him twice that it was me and not the food when he expressed concern over my uneaten meal, and refusing his offer of take-home boxes for it. There was no point, when any food I brought home from a lunch with Rebecca would doubtless suffer the same fate as the elaborate fruit and nut platter had.

The server departed with our dishes, continuing to cast frowning looks over his shoulder on his way back to the kitchen, and I returned to my conversation with Rebecca. But not the innately good part, because the interruption had given me a chance to sift through my many questions in favor of the ones that were more pressing—and less personal.

"So, if Drummond's tower was destroyed," I said, "what happened to the stones?"

"We think they're traveling with Drummond at the moment," Rebecca replied. "Now that Morok is out of the picture—"

"Wait. Out of the picture how?"

"The portal, of course."

"The portal *succeeded*?" I asked the question far too loudly, and a half dozen nearby diners looked over at our table, some with frowns of annoyance, others with surprise—and a curiosity I didn't think was healthy for any of us. I dropped my voice to a hiss. "Morok succeeded in creating a portal to one of the splinters? But how?"

"That magick is beyond us," the Mage admitted. "We believe the Crones were somehow involved, but we don't know how. We only know that Morok is gone, and Drummond is set on taking his place, and he's not taking any chances with letting the stones out of his sight."

"Taking his—" I dropped the question I had about Crones —along with my jaw—and blinked at her. Twice. "You mean, he wants to be a *god*?"

Rebecca rolled her eyes. "You don't think he's always wanted that?"

Fair point. But still ...

I mustered my many ping-pong balls of thought as best I could. "Can he? I mean, is that even possible?"

"With the way his following is growing?" She snorted softly, as if the answer was obvious.

"What does his following have to do with it?"

"You of all people should know that belief holds a great deal of power, Sister Monica. And a great many people believe in Drummond. With five stones already in his possession, if he gets his hands on that"—she nodded in the direction of my stone-holding fist under the table—"and the alien, the power of their collective belief is absolutely enough to elevate him to god. *That* is what we're trying to prevent."

Her answer struck like a blade of ice to my very core, and for a second, even my ping-pong thoughts froze, because sweet Mary Magdalene, she was serious. I wanted to argue with her, to tell her that it was impossible and no one could just *become* a god because people believed in him, but ...

But history and humanity, I thought with blinding insight, may have already proved me wrong. Many times over. Because if magick was real but kept suppressed, and someone learned how to manipulate it, and others saw their powers as miraculous, then—

"Morok," I croaked. "Is that how—"

"The Slavic god of darkness," Rebecca said, an amused twinkle in her eye telling me that she was quite enjoying watching my brain melt. "Also the Egyptian gods, the Greek gods, the Celtic gods ..."

"Jesus," I muttered as she trailed off.

"Him, too."

I ignored the obvious bait, working my way through far more information than I'd wanted—or was healthy for me, I was convinced. Drummond wanted the stones and

Methuselah so he could be a god? Because needing them myself in order to save the Weaver hadn't been enough pressure?

Not that anything Rebecca had told me had changed that. It had changed *me*, perhaps, but not what I had to do. Or how I planned to do it.

"Where?" I asked.

It was only a single word, but Rebecca knew what I meant. A little cat-that-swallowed-the-cream smile played across her lips, because she knew she'd won, too.

Well. She thought she had.

I was just better at hiding my own smile.

"He's slated to be the keynote speaker on Monday at the Global Economic Forum in Ottawa," she told me, "which will be funded by the consortium, of course."

"And which you'll be attending," I said. "Of course."

The Mage's expression didn't change, and the phrase *poker face* came to mind. "We have a vested interested in the topic of world economics, yes."

I let slide the unspoken challenge. I was not, I told myself firmly, going to engage in a discussion about her group's *interests*. Did I have questions about their idea of economics? Absolutely. Did I already know the answers to those questions, given the ilk of their collective? Most likely. Would I be able to change her mind through any kind of discourse? I held back a snort at the very idea.

The fact that she was a Mage at all meant she'd bought into the patriarchy that was at the root of their kind. Whether she'd done it for her own power or for perceived safety—or both—she'd abandoned every principle for which I stood: integrity, equity … humanity itself.

Come to think of it, her unwillingness to attack Drummond's condo in New York had likely been more about optics and saving their group's skin than about any sort of conscience regarding the populace. Much better to send a solitary, aging woman to do their dirty work for them here in Canada.

This alliance just kept getting better and better. But at least I had a location, and that had to count for something. I just had to get to Ottawa. Surely it wouldn't be all that difficult, especially compared with having to cross the border into the States.

Although taking the train would be out of the question. I held back a shudder. After the trip up to Quebec City from Kingston—and the Mage attack on it—I had no intention of making myself a sitting duck in a metal tube again. I was sure the nuns would have other ideas for travel, perhaps with the help of others in the Obsidian Sisterhood, and we had—I did a quick mental count of the days and decided that today was most likely Friday, which meant we had only the weekend to get me there.

And even if we succeeded, I still faced a whole other problem, because while I might arrive in time for the forum, I didn't know how long it would take me to locate the stones, get them away from Drummond, and—

Well. What happened then remained to be seen. The point was that the week Drummond had allotted to Talia was running out fast.

"One week, and one week only," his voice echoed in my mind. *"After that, we send one body part per day until you comply. If you continue to defy us and this particular body does not survive, we will take another of you. And then another. And then another."*

One week. Assuming he'd meant the seven-day kind and not just five business days, we were already down by two— three by end of day today. The consortium might well remove the first part of Talia before I so much as laid eyes on the stones, never mind hands.

"You have to rescue her first," I said abruptly.

Rebecca stared. "I beg your pardon?"

"Talia. You have to get her away from the consortium before I go after the stones. Otherwise, the deal is off."

"That isn't what we agreed to—"

"Fuck the agreement," I snapped. "They will take her apart piece by piece if I don't agree to *their* terms, and they will send those pieces to me, do you understand? You either stop them, or I walk."

Rebecca heaved a martyred-sounding sigh and reached a hand under the table. I tensed, and the stone's webs stirred against my palm. They subsided again as the Mage pulled out a cell phone and set it flat on the table. She tapped the screen a few times, then turned it around and slid it toward me to reveal a photo of a woman standing in front of a huge, soaring window with a stunning city view beyond it.

My gaze zeroed in on the woman's face, brown-skinned and unsmiling, her hair pulled back tightly. Familiar dark eyes stared back at me, the lines around them etched a little more deeply than I remembered. She looked thinner than I remembered, too. Thinner and wearier, but still unmistakably alive. Unmistakably defiant. Unmistakably Talia.

And then I noticed the city behind her. Modern and unfamiliar except for ... that. I caught my breath and snatched the phone from an unresisting Rebecca. I pinched my thumb and finger together on the image, then spread them apart to zoom in on it. Talia disappeared except for her left shoulder, above which, far in the background, sat the familiar profile of the Chateau Frontenac that overlooked Old Quebec.

This time, the stone's webs unfurled through my veins to coil in my chest alongside a flare of rage. The Mage and her collective had already rescued her. They'd rescued her, and—

"You *have* her already?" I snarled. "You have her, and you didn't tell me?"

The phone's screen blinked off, stealing the image of my friend from me. I suppressed the urge to shove it into Rebecca's hand and demand she reopen it. Or to throttle her. Both were valid responses, in my opinion, but the Mage was speaking, and I forced myself to pay attention and not indulge in wild speculation about where Talia was being held.

So near, I thought. *I never dreamed she'd be so near. I thought they'd take her away, as far from us as they could.*

"We have her under surveillance," Rebecca corrected. "We know where she is, and we know that she's safe."

"If you know where she is, then you can take her from them."

"And then what?" The Mage reached across and plucked her phone away from me. "Do you really think the consortium will just let her go without some kind of backlash? You're smarter than that, Mon—Sister Monica."

She was right. I knew she was right. Drummond's message had said so. "*If you continue to defy us … we will take another of you. And then another. And then another.*"

A wave of impotence swamped me, and I gritted my teeth.

Across the table, Rebecca Monterey sighed and, with an edge of impatience to her voice, said, "We won't let anything happen to her. The one who sent me the picture"—she waved the phone aloft—"is one of ours. She will step in if they try to carry out their threat."

So. Another *she* had bought into the Mage mentality. Was there no limit to the patriarchal brainwashing that went on? A little voice in the back of my head snorted at the question, because history in and of itself had answered that—many, many times over.

Gritting my teeth, I wrestled rage and webs into submission, pulling the latter back from where they had snaked across the table beneath the tablecloth. Rebecca's gaze flicked toward the rippling white linen, and the lines around her eyes tightened, but she made no comment.

Then, just as my hand relaxed its grip on the stone again, a new thought occurred to me, bringing a sudden wash of horror in its wake. Because sweet Mary Magdalene, what if

I'd been worrying about the wrong Mages watching the monastery? If the consortium was already here, in Quebec City, what was to stop them from grabbing Phoenix and Methuselah right now? While I was—

Fucking hell. I'd left them unprotected but for the nuns and the paltry few Molotov cocktails they'd built since they'd used up their supply at the Citadelle.

CHAPTER 13

I scrambled out from the banquette seat, panic running like liquid fire through my veins, but Rebecca's voice stopped me as I whirled, poised for flight.

"Relax," she said. "Your friends are safe. There's no sign of the consortium in the city other than the ones holding that one"—she indicated her phone—"and we have people watching the monastery just in case."

The reassurance did little to ease the fear gripping my lungs, because first, after the beating I'd seen her group take at the Citadelle, her assurance meant diddly squat if the consortium sent in their troops, and second, I didn't care whose Mages were watching the monastery, there were *Mages watching the monastery*.

"We have no intention of letting Methuselah fall into consortium hands," she said, as if she'd read my mind on the first part. "There are a great many more of us here than were at the Citadelle, and the goliath is no longer an issue. You have my word that we won't let anything happen to your friends. Any of them."

I would have liked to know more about how the goliath was no longer an issue, but I was too busy scowling at the idea of a Mage's word. What exactly, I wondered, was that worth, anyway?

Again, Rebecca seemed to sense my thoughts. She slid out from her own banquette seat far more elegantly than I had. Smoothing down the skirt of her dress, she lifted her chin and faced me with squared shoulders and haughty brown eyes, as if offended that I could even dream of doubting her.

"I told you before," she reminded me icily, "that my word is my bond."

With great effort, I refrained from raising a skeptical brow. Or from drawling the *sure* that sat on the tip of my tongue.

"Now," she continued. "Do we have an agreement?"

I pulled myself together, mustered all the calm I could eke out of my depths and, in a voice as flat as hers had been testy, said, "What about security at the forum?"

"They're the consortium," she said. "And Drummond is aiming for god status, remember? He won't have security beyond his own."

Mages. Mages would be their security, and I would have to get past them twice—once on my way in, and again on my way out with the stones. The only thing I'd have in my favor would be the element of surprise, because Drummond, bless his dark, shriveled little heart, wouldn't be expecting me to attack him on their own turf. He was arrogant enough to think that I—a mere woman, no less—would be sitting and waiting for him to tell me when to jump.

"And when I have the stones?" I asked Rebecca. "How do I reach you?"

"We will know," she said. "And we will contact you to arrange the exchange. Your friend for the stones, and you keep the alien. As agreed."

She extended a hand toward me in a seal-the-deal gesture, but I refused to dignify it with so much as a glance. Turning my back on her, I started toward the exit. Her voice followed me.

"And you, Sister Monica?" she challenged. "Is your word your bond, too?"

Without pause or hesitation, I looked over my shoulder, met her gaze squarely, and inclined my head.

"Always," I said.

At least, it was when I actually gave it.

Stiff-spined determination carried me out of the restaurant and through the hotel lobby to the double-doored entrance. Well, that and a healthy dose of pride, if I were to be entirely honest. But whatever. The important things were that I left without looking back, that I didn't collapse in a heap on the floor under the weight of everything Rebecca had told me, and that I didn't pitch the stone as far away from me as I could.

Or turn tail and run in the opposite direction.

Because holy Mother of All, how I wanted to.

Stopping in the space between the two sets of doors, I sucked in a quivering breath and tried to wrap my scarf around my face again. It was no easy task with the stone gripped in one hand—or with my brain skidding left and right and up and down and entirely unable to focus on the task.

And the hard stare I could feel focused between my shoulder blades.

I finally got the scarf wrapped well enough to hold it in place. The final result was loose and lopsided and would keep me nowhere near as warm as Sister Lise's handiwork, but it would have to do. I went to work on the coat buttons next, and then tugged on my toque and mittens. Then, tucking my hands into my pockets and still refusing to look behind me, I shouldered through the door and onto the sidewalk.

Somehow, I made it around the corner of the hotel without faltering. That, however, was as far as my determination would carry me. A blast of wind rocketed down the narrow street, rattling the cheerful Christmas greenery and bows in the window boxes lining the building and stealing my breath—and, along with it, all the bravado that had carried me through the ordeal with Rebecca.

The full impact of the responsibility facing me landed like an avalanche across my shoulders, complete with icy pellets driven by the wind against my unprotected face. An avalanche of responsibility and words and information and magickal facts that I hadn't anticipated and could never have imagined. I put a hand out to the stone wall beside me, digging mittened fingers against it to keep from dropping to my knees.

Gods and portals, slivers of Earth, multiverses, midwitches, Crones … what in the name of Mary Magdalene herself was I supposed to do with all of that? With any of it? The sheer … monumentalness … of it.

A group of pedestrians approached, talking and laughing and stopping to take a selfie in front of the brightly decorated window box I leaned beside. They were young and vibrant and giddy and carefree, and so far removed from my own reality that I felt as if I were watching from a distance … or through the eyes of an alien. This was how Methuselah must have felt, I thought. Perhaps for thousands of years.

Perhaps even now.

One of the young men, bespectacled and with peach fuzz instead of a mustache, stepped on my toes, and the female companion hanging off his arm jostled my shoulder as they crowded past—both without apology, oblivious to me—and then the group moved on around the corner, leaving the sidewalk empty, and me … emptier.

A frisson of fear slithered down my spine. No, not fear. Doubt.

Well. Doubt *and* fear. And something else. Something bigger and darker and—

Another gust of wind, funneled by the narrow street, buffeted against me. I stepped out of it and into the shelter of a recessed doorway on the side of the hotel I'd left. A hand-lettered sign was tacked to the inside of the glass, with instructions I couldn't read and an arrow pointing to the right. I hoped that meant no one would come barreling through it for the next few minutes, because I really, really needed a place to catch my breath and regroup.

Shivering, I plunged my hands into my coat pockets and burrowed my chin into the loose scarf. My faint panic remained, not all of it attributable to Phoenix and Methuselah and the anxiously waiting nuns. No, it was more than that. I felt … alone, I thought. Apart. Separate not just from them, but from everything. Everything except the stone, solid in my right hand, and the darkness that permeated me.

I shuddered. Perhaps it was the stress of … well, everything, or maybe it was just an overactive imagination, but for the first time, I swore I could sense it moving within me, like the living thing that Methuselah claimed it to be. Moving in my veins, my bones, my muscles, my every cell.

As if it was taking over.

Fuck.

I drew a deep, desperate breath, focusing on the cold of the air rushing through my nostrils, following its path down my throat and into my lungs and belly, and then concentrating on the warmth of its exhale. The panic in me released a tiny corner of my mind. I took another breath, slower this time. Less desperate. Then I held it as I purposefully, intentionally paused.

My thoughts, my insecurities, my doubts, my responsibilities, even my attempts at remaining calm and centered … I paused it all, and then—then I breathed again.

I just breathed.

Just was.

And then, because I was also just human, I slumped against the wall, slid down to sit on the frozen, unused hotel doorstep, and quietly folded in on myself under the weight of simply too much.

WHEN I LIFTED MY HEAD FROM MY KNEES, I WAS STARTLED TO find that the daylight was gone. I stared across the street at a light that had come on in a second-floor window, then leaned forward to let my gaze travel the long building made up of many row houses. Red and white string lights lined a doorway half a block away on the other side of the street; multicolored ones twinkled around the windows of the row house beside it, and street lamps had come on in both directions. All of them visible because it was … dark?

Connection, memory, responsibility … everything that had occupied my mind just seconds before disappeared in a flash of panic and a dozen questions.

How the hell could it be dark? How long had I been sitting here? What time was it, any—

The church bell I'd heard chime once—seemingly moments before—pealed again, and I paused to count. One, two, three, four … *five*? I'd been gone from the monastery for —I did another mental count—almost seven hours? Sweet Mary Magdalene, the sisters and Phoenix would be beside themselves with worry by now, and Methuselah—

Damn. Now *I* was sick with worry. If Rebecca had Mages, plural, watching the monastery as she'd said, Methuselah would have sensed them there. He'd be going mad. I had to get home. *Now.*

I planted my hands on either side of myself and pushed to my—

I tried to plant my hands on either side—

I tugged at my hands and—

Fucking hell.

I stopped moving and took stock of my situation. My knees were still drawn up to my chest, and my hands, despite my best, determined efforts, were still wedged between them and my torso. I tried to straighten out my legs, but they, too, refused to cooperate, feeling as if they were locked in place. Fresh panic gripped me, but then I frowned. The whisper of another memory slipped into my mind, and understanding gelled beside it.

Ah hell, I thought. Again?

Then I sighed. It was hardly my favorite way to wake up, but on the bright side, at least I'd been here before. When I'd come to on the banks of the Chaudière River after the train incident, I'd been in a similar cocoon, although I hadn't been able to see out of that one the way I could now. This one appeared to end at my neck. I could still move my head and see the world beyond my little doorway, which meant that I could probably call for help, too. But as quickly as the idea arose, I discarded it. First, because of the explaining I would have to do, and second, I wasn't sure who would come to my aid.

No, it would be tedious, but I knew what to do, and I'd get myself out of my predicament. Focusing all my attention on the fingertips of one hand, I coaxed them into the shape of a tiny claw, then picked away at the cocoon with them, scraping persistently at a single small spot. I felt more annoyance at the delay than fear, although that didn't entirely subside. How could it, when I'd seen so many other cocoons go …

Well. *Horribly wrong* would be an understatement.

This, however, was just the stone trying to keep me safe, and damned if a glimmer of gratitude wasn't edging out the annoyance. I swallowed a snort, because also damned if this relationship the stone and I had wasn't turning into some kind of bizarre symbiosis—I fed it, it protected me, and together we played whack-a-Mage.

Another swallowed snort, this one containing a touch of hysteria at the path my thoughts had taken. *Whack-a-Mage? Really?* I mean, it wasn't wrong, but sweet Mary Magdalene, I was beginning to think I'd sat here so long that my brain had frozen.

And short-circuited.

I scraped harder at the cocoon—also frozen—until, at last, my numb fingertips broke through. A moment later, I'd freed one hand and, from there, it became easier. Chunks of ice-hardened spiderwebs fell away from me as I broke them off, shattering on the stones beside me.

By the time I freed my feet, I was sweating beneath my winter layers. The warmth I'd created in myself didn't extend to my joints, however, and hoisting myself up from the hard stone portico required a mighty effort and much muttering under my breath. I had definitely been out here for too long. *And* I'd neglected my workouts for too long.

Symbiosis be damned. I was becoming reliant on the stone to keep me moving—that was *not* good.

It took several more minutes to free myself completely. The traffic along the street had all but evaporated, and apart from a taxi driving past, nothing and no one moved along the block. I hadn't quite decided whether that was a good thing (spiderweb explanation-wise) or a bad one—because I really could have used a hand, especially with the getting off the ground part. But regardless, at last I was upright.

I lurched down to the sidewalk and began shuffling, then walking, then striding with purpose as my knees and hips slowly got on board with the idea of movement. If I was going to be in Ottawa by Monday—I needed to hustle.

My brain had begun functioning again along with the rest of me, and now it was making up for lost time as I walked, sorting through the mountain of logistics facing me. Because I wouldn't be going to Ottawa alone. I had no choice but to take Methuselah and Phoenix with me, because I didn't dare leave them here with the nuns.

Or, more precisely, with Rebecca's flunkies.

It wasn't because I thought I could protect either of them

from the consortium better than the flunkies could, but because I couldn't protect them from the flunkies themselves when I betrayed the alliance Rebecca thought she and I had made. So yes, Phoenix and Methuselah would be coming with me, but how? And where would I put them to keep them safe when I went after the stones? And—

I turned the corner into the little street leading to the monastery and skidded to a halt so quickly that I almost fell into a snowbank. My astonished gaze traveled the street and the buildings lining it, briefly alighting on one stranger after another after another.

Mages. Multiples of Mages. Fucking dozens of Mages.

They were everywhere. Watching from windows and rooftops, sitting in cars, walking dogs, taking out garbage cans to the curb, looking no different from ordinary citizens except for the fact that every single one of their gazes had locked onto me.

Well, that and the unmistakable energy that crackled between them and made the edges of the stone bite into my hand.

"Run!" Methuselah's voice screamed in my head, and it took everything I had not to do just that. For long, interminable seconds, I stood frozen under their stares. I was afraid to even breathe lest I inadvertently start a war (assuming they all belonged to Rebecca) or, worse, had stumbled into one (if some of them belonged to the consortium). As quickly as the latter idea formed, I dismissed it. If that were the case, I would already be at the center of a full-blown battle, not just standing at the side of a little Quebec side street wrapped in snow and silence.

I took a breath. Then another. Then, my own gaze flicking from Mage-in-car to Mage-on-rooftop to Mage-with-French-bulldog-in-a-bright-red-sweater, I began a slow advance toward the opening into the courtyard of the monastery.

It was like walking a gauntlet.

CHAPTER 14

MY heart was thundering in my ears and my breath coming in gasps by the time I banged on the wooden door with no door handle in our agreed-upon signal. *"Knock three times,"* Sister Simonne had told me when I'd left for the hotel, *"like the song."*

With the gazes of Mages tracking my every move, I was astounded that I remembered.

I was even more astounded when Sister Simonne opened the door a mere crack, reached through to grab my arm, and dragged me into the utter pandemonium that had become the monastery, before slamming the door shut again and barring it with her bulk.

"We're having a moment!" she shouted at me over the chaos.

I could see that.

Standing in the entry, my toes like blocks of ice in my boots and my nerves still scraped raw by the gauntlet outside, I gaped at the scene before me. Sisters Bernadette and Lise were both trying to catch and soothe a frantic Methuselah, who was pacing back and forth shrieking, *"Run!"* at the top of his lungs. Sister Colette, her mouth set in a grim line, doggedly kept pace with him, blocking the way to the door with her walker. And Phoenix—

My gaze darted past the melee to the corridor beyond, and then up the stairs. Phoenix was nowhere to be seen. Panic flared in me, and I whirled to Sister Simonne. She held a hand up and answered my question before I'd uttered it.

"She's fine," she yelled. "There was a little … incident … with Methuselah. We sent her into the living room."

Incident … Methuselah. My blood cooled to roughly the

same temperature as my toes, and I looked over my shoulder toward the living room.

Sister Simonne tapped me on the shoulder and yelled again, "She's fine! Really! But that—"

She nodded past me to where Methuselah's shrieks were increasing in both pitch and frequency, becoming a steady, unrelenting stream of, "*Run run run run run!*"

Not to mention a skull-piercing one.

Sweet Mary Magdalene, he was loud. I clapped my mittened hands over my ears, trying to block out some of the sound, to think. There had to be a way to stop him—*what kind of incident between him and Phoenix?*—some way to get through to him—*had he hurt her?*—some way to reassure—*but no, Sister Simonne said she's okay*—

"*Runrunrunrunrun!*" screeched Methuselah.

My last wire-taut nerve snapped.

"Jesus *fuck!*" I bellowed.

It was like I'd hit a switch. Silence dropped over the entire group—screeching alien included—so fast that it took me a moment to even recognize it. Another for the relief to kick in. A third to realize what I'd said … done … oh, shit.

I took my hands from my ears and, one by one, met the shocked—no, stunned—gazes of the nuns. The full magnitude of how far I might have overstepped settled over me. I mean, the Ursulines were spectacularly liberal as far as nuns went, but even they would have limits—backed by decades of religious discipline—and I was pretty sure I'd just crossed every single one of them.

Fuck, I thought.

But before I could apologize, Methuselah turned and bolted down the corridor toward the kitchen, sisters Lise and Bernadette in full chase. Sister Colette brought up the rear with her walker, muttering, "*Tabarnak*," under her breath.

I watched them go, torn between running after them and crawling into a corner somewhere. I settled for turning to

Sister Simonne. "I'm so, *so* sorry," I said. "I don't know what came over me, saying that. I—"

"Are you kidding?" Sister Simonne pushed away from the door she'd been guarding and wrapped me in a bear hug. "Do you have any idea how long he's been going on like that? If it weren't for these old stone walls, we would have had every single neighbor calling the police, I'm sure."

"But," I wheezed, "but you all looked so shocked."

"We were," she replied, "but not because of what you said —trust me, the whole lot of us have said much worse. We're shocked because you did the impossible and shut him up. So *thank you*."

She gave me another squeeze, curtailing my ability to respond at all this time as the remainder of the air in my lungs *oof*ed from me. Then she set me away from her and looked me up and down with a mildly horrified expression.

"Good heavens," she said, "you're still wearing your coat and boots. Come on, let's get you out of them." Briskly, she stripped off my mittens and tossed them aside, but before her fingers had done more than touch the top button of the heavy wool coat, another body wedged between us and yet more arms tried to squeeze the air from me.

"You're alive!" exclaimed Phoenix. "Thank god ... or whatever it is that I'm supposed to believe in!"

Sister Simonne chortled and patted her on the back. "God will do just fine," she said. "It's the thought that counts."

I thought it was funny—perhaps because of oxygen deprivation—but Phoenix ignored her, pushed me to arm's length, then pulled me back in for another hug.

"Where *were* you?" she scolded. "It's been *hours.* We were worried—and then Methuselah started screaming, and—" She pulled back, her wide, haunted blue eyes searching mine. A scorch mark blackened her right cheek, and I inhaled sharply. Was that what Sister Simonne had meant by an incident with Methuselah? Before I could ask, Phoenix was talking again.

"So?" she demanded. "Did you see her? The Mage, I mean? Did you make a deal with her? Can she really rescue Talia?"

Sister Simonne tutted and gently but forcibly moved the young woman aside. "Let the poor woman at least take off her coat," she chided, "and then we need to get something warm into her. She's half frozen and exhausted, and—"

I cut her off to answer Phoenix's question, because the young woman's peace of mind was more important than my boots or coat or how cold or tired I might be. Far more important. "She already has," I told her. "At least, almost. One of her Mages is a mole in the consortium—one of Talia's guards —and they're holding her somewhere here, in Quebec. Rebecca showed me a picture of her, and I could see the Chateau in the background."

But instead of eliciting the relief and happiness I expected, my response triggered two entirely different things: first, a look of utter horror from Sister Simonne as she put a hand to her breast and staggered back to lean on the wall; and second, a sudden dissolving into tears from Phoenix, who also sagged against the wall.

I stared back and forth between them, utterly nonplussed.

"He's right," Sister Simonne croaked. "Methuselah is right —the consortium is here. I have to tell the others!"

"Wait," I said, putting an arm out to block her path to the kitchen. "It's not what you—" I broke off, distracted by Phoenix tugging on my arm—and by the hope shining from behind the tears in her blue eyes.

"This changes everything, right?" she demanded.

I blinked at her, not following, and Sister Simonne stopped trying to dodge my arm to do likewise. "Pardon?" I said.

"I said, this changes everything, right?" Like quicksilver, the young woman's expression went from hopeful to thoughtful to frowning to eager and then, without waiting, she answered her own question. "It does. Because if Rebecca Monterey knows where Talia is being kept, we can take her. We can get her back—*now*."

"Hold on, Phoenix," I began, but she was on a roll now and paid no attention to me.

"We have to go after her," she announced. She fished a tissue from her hoodie pocket and swiped it under her nose, then tucked it away again, practically dancing on the spot in her excitement. "Today. Now. Before that Monterey woman leaves. We'll go to the hotel, and you can make her tell us where Talia is—make her give her to us."

I made another effort. "I wish it was that simp—"

"It is," she interrupted fiercely. She stopped dancing and glared at me. "It's exactly that simple! We take Talia from them and then she's safe, and we can find somewhere to hide, and you don't have to go after those stupid stones, wherever they are, and then—and then—"

She broke off, floundering, and for the second time that day, something in me snapped. But this time, it was something ugly.

"And then *what*?" I snarled. "What the fuck do you suggest we do then, Phoenix? Hole up somewhere and wait for the consortium *and* Rebecca's Mages to come for us? Or maybe we should stay here, so we can throw exploding bottles at them. All while we wait to see if Methuselah is right, and then we can watch the entire damned world unravel, but at least we'll be together. Is that the idea? Is that what you want?"

My words were harsh. Angry. Unforgivable. And as uncharacteristic as me collapsing for hours on a winter sidewalk. A quiet kind of panic bubbled up in my core. Sweet Mary Magdalene, I was well and truly losing it, wasn't I? I'd never spoken to Phoenix like this before. I'd never spoken to anyone like this. I hadn't known I could—and I hated discovering it was possible.

What made it worse was knowing that Phoenix's own anger stemmed from fear—I'd seen this kind of reaction countless times before in traumatized women, and I knew that Phoenix had seen her fair share of trauma. She'd lost so much in her life, and she was terrified, and I … I was older and wiser and supposed to be caring for her.

But even as I watched her beloved face crumple in hurt and then darken with fury, there was a part of me that didn't care. That was just too damned tired to care, even as I watched the young woman I'd come to think of as a daughter spin on her heel and bolt up the stairs, leaving me with a silent Sister Simonne … and the stone.

The goddamn, fucking stone, whose weight dragged at me like gravity magnified a thousand times, and whose spider strands sought to wind around my heart and lungs and to steal inside my brain, reaching for the darkness that lurked there. The darkness that had surfaced with a vengeance.

The darkness that never left me, that was—calming and centering aside—slowly taking me over.

Exhaustion crept over me. The innate good that Rebecca Monterey had spoken of in me—which I thought at the time might be the magick keeping me safe from the stone— suddenly seemed like a distant concept that had slipped from my grasp and drifted beyond my reach. I hadn't even asked Phoenix about the incident with Methuselah, because I hadn't cared enough about that, either.

How easy would it be, a distant part of me wondered, to just stop caring altogether?

Sister Simonne's hand settled onto my arm. "Are you all right?" she asked.

Her touch brought me up short. The compassion behind it sliced like a blade through the webs trying to consume me, and something tiny and solid and stubborn stirred in my core, pushing back against the despair.

Meeting Sister Simonne's gentle gaze, I swallowed a sob,

turning it into a hiccup as I pressed the fingers of my hand over my mouth. I would *not* cry, I told myself fiercely. First of all, I had nothing to cry about—unlike Phoenix—and second, if I was going to do this, if I was even going to *attempt* doing this, I had no time for tears or pity parties.

The nun turned me to face her. "She'll come around," she said, starting on the oversized black buttons of my coat. "She's just—"

"Scared?" I interrupted roughly. "I know that. But—"

"I was going to say overcompensating," Sister Simonne said gently.

I frowned down at her. "Overcompensating? For what?"

"Talia. Their relationship was …"

She let her sentence trail off, letting her words settle into me. My frown deepened as I thought back to the many clashes between the young woman and the police detective. They'd managed to coexist because of the circumstances—and because of me, I suspected. Sometimes I'd even detected a hint of reluctant mutual respect between them, but their relationship had been about what one would expect between a hardened cop and a young woman with a juvenile record for computer hacking who lived in a shelter … and happened to be Trans.

"It was tense," I agreed, "but if you're saying Phoenix feels guilty because Talia was kidnapped, that makes no sense."

"How does any of this make sense?" Sister Simonne undid the last of the buttons and slid the coat from my shoulders as she might have done for a child. "One of the two people she has left in the world is being held by Mages, and the other is planning to attack other, possibly more powerful Mages to save the first."

The nun hung the coat on one of the hooks lining the wall behind the door, then knelt to untie my boots. "She needs reassurance, Sister Monica," she said, looking up at me with equal parts recrimination, sadness, and—

Damn it, there was that compassion again. My eyes filled with tears for a second time.

"From you," she added.

My tears evaporated in a fresh tug of spiderwebs across my heart, because I knew that. I just had none to give.

Using the wall as a brace, I slipped off one boot and then the other. Then, without letting myself respond to either the nun or her compassion, I walked away, my gaze fixed on the kitchen door and my attention on what waited for me beyond it.

The other nuns. The relating of my meeting with Rebecca and the decision I'd come to. The formulation of a plan. Methuselah.

But not Phoenix.

CHAPTER 15

Guilt followed me into the kitchen and stood at my shoulder like a shadow of the darkness itself. I pretended not to notice it—or the ragged hole in my heart where a piece of it had torn away from me to follow Phoenix in my stead.

Would she know that? Probably not, but perhaps Sister Simonne, who had started up the stairs as I reached the kitchen door, would tell her. Or I could try to tell her later. But right now, I had too much to impart to the nuns, Methuselah's sporadic yelps of "Run!" had started up again, and—perhaps most important of all—I wasn't sure I could be trusted to be the person she needed at the moment.

Frankly, I wasn't sure that person even existed anymore, but that was a whole other issue, one that I would also deal with later. For now, I had work to do. Work that I was going to need help with—but first, it appeared that my help might need help.

Sister Lise had her back turned to me as she filled a kettle at the sink, but sisters Bernadette and Colette were hovering over an agitated Methuselah in the far corner of the kitchen. He'd taken refuge on the floor in the corner by the utility closet, hugging his knees to himself and rocking back and forth. I started toward the little group, but Sister Bernadette glanced over her shoulder and gave me a tiny shake of her head. They either had this under control, or they thought that my "help" would be anything but.

Which, given my earlier outburst, was entirely valid.

I shuffled to the table, pulled out a chair, and lowered my aching body into it. As well dressed for winter as I'd been—and as much protection as the webs had given me—the cold had seeped into my very bones, settling into all the injuries that had been inflicted on me—or that I'd inflicted on myself. I flexed the ankle I'd fractured in my voluntary leap down into the deep trench at the Citadelle. The stone's webs may have welded everything together, but magick or no magick, my no-longer-thirty-year-old body didn't bounce as well as it once had.

And sweet Mary Magdalene, it had opinions on the abuse it was taking at this stage of life.

I shifted my sit-bones on the hard chair, crossed and uncrossed my ankles beneath it, rolled my shoulders forward and back, and then, with a sigh, gave up on my attempts to find comfort. Resting my elbows on the table and my chin against my hands, the fingers of one covering the fist—yes, with the stone still inside—of the other, I watched Sister Bernadette on her knees beside Methuselah, near him but not touching as she murmured words that were too quiet for me to hear.

Sister Colette, leaning on her walker beside them, nodded her head in rhythmic agreement with whatever the other nun was saying. The alien man-child continued to rock back and forth, but blessedly, his warnings of "Run!" were diminishing in volume.

I turned my head toward the lace-covered window beside the table and the frozen night beyond it and, for a moment, let my mind just … drift. Was one of Rebecca's Mages watching outside this window, too? Probably. And probably more than one.

Huh. I kept thinking of them as *her* Mages, but was that really true? Unlikely, I mused, but possible, because for the patriarchy to have grown to the extremes that it had, there had to have been more than simple, passive acceptance from women. There had to have been active participation, too. Female leaders who'd bought into the whole male dominance idea and furthered that agenda for whatever reasons of their own. Although I'd have to question whether they were true leaders in those instances. More like carefully molded puppets who were allowed to perform on behalf of their masters.

Which seemed the more likely scenario for Rebecca Monterey.

That whole line of thinking was downright depressing. Even if we—*I*—somehow succeeded in getting the stones away from the consortium, keeping them out of Rebecca's hands, and saving the mysterious Weaver that Methuselah had talked about—after I found her, of course—it would be only the beginning. We would still have *so* much work ahead of us.

See? Depressing.

I closed my eyes and switched my thoughts to Talia, letting myself, for the first time since leaving Rebecca at the hotel, sink into the knowledge that she was still alive. That she wasn't going to be dismantled piece by piece. A shuddering sigh unfolded in my chest, and I squeezed my eyelids together against the threatening tears.

Phoenix didn't know it, but sweet Mary Magdalene, I understood her impulsive desire to just go after our friend, to force Rebecca to hand her over and damn the consequences. A part of me wanted to do the same. With every fiber of my being, I wanted it. I wanted Talia here, with us, safe within these solid stone walls that had stood against so much. After all the Toronto police detective had done, all that she'd given up to help get me this far and keep Phoenix safe, she deserved so much better than to be a pawn in this potentially catastrophic game that the Mages played.

And I knew I could do it, too. I knew I was powerful enough, knew I could force Rebecca's hand and make her return Talia now, alliance be damned. Except, if Methuselah was to be believed—and I did believe him—Talia was only one pawn among billions. Billions of people, billions of stars, billions of galaxies that all deserved better. That all deserved a chance.

Therein lay my struggle—and my increasingly tenuous

grasp on that innate goodness that Rebecca had talked about. Because if I saved one over all, if I saved my friend, would it be out of goodness or to salve my own conscience? And if I didn't save her—if I did what I was thinking of doing and deliberately turned my back on her—what would happen then to the good in me?

My fist tightened around the stone. And then there was the whole question of who I thought I was to do any of this at all. The very idea of being caught up in something this big, this cosmic—of being central to it—was beyond audacious. It was arrogant beyond measure, placing me on a level not with the people I tried to serve but with those who tried to rule the entire world.

Fucking hell, what was I thinking?

I was on the verge of pushing back my chair and bolting from the room—although to where, I had no idea—when a small *thunk* sounded on the table. Opening my eyes, I looked down to see Sister Bernadette sliding a glass of amber liquid across the table toward me.

"For medicinal purposes," she said. "You look like you need it."

She'd get no argument from me on that.

I glanced over to where Sister Colette still kept a watchful eye on Methuselah, who had finally calmed down. That made one of us. Sister Lise had disappeared from the kitchen, probably in search of Sister Simonne and Phoenix. I flinched away from the memory of my anger and reached for the glass.

Oh yes. I definitely needed a drink.

I took a sip, and a fiery liquid slipped across my tongue and down my throat. Whiskey. I'd only had it a handful of times in my life, but I recognized the taste. Whether a connoisseur would have considered it a good one or not, I couldn't have said, but the warmth pooling in my belly was comforting, and that was all that mattered. That, and the distraction it provided.

"Better?" Sister Bernadette asked, taking a seat beside me.

I held back a snicker, because she was kidding, right? I took another swig of distraction as the kitchen door swung open to admit sisters Lise and Simonne …

But no Phoenix.

Shit. I took another sip of whiskey. Then I looked around the kitchen, my glance encompassing all the nuns. It was time to stop wasting time.

CHAPTER 16

"Drummond keeps the stones with him at all times," I said without preamble. "He's going to be in Ottawa for an economic forum on Monday. I need a plan to get me there—me, Phoenix, and Methuselah."

Silence met my announcement. Not unexpected, but … not quite *as* expected, either, I thought, seeing the swift, unspoken exchange that took place between the nuns. A tightening of Sister Bernadette's lips, a tiny shake of Sister Simonne's shoulders, a twitch of Sister Colette's brow, a sideways flicker of Sister Lise's eyes.

I wasn't sure what it was about, but before I asked my own questions, I needed to answer the many I knew they had. I gestured to sisters Simonne and Lise to join us, and they crossed over to the table. Along the way, Sister Lise paused to switch off the burner beneath the kettle she'd placed on the stove a few minutes before. Looking over at Sister Colette, I raised an eyebrow in invitation, but she shook her head.

Her frown had deepened.

Ignoring it, I gave my glass a swirl, assembled my thoughts, and launched into a summary of my meeting with Rebecca Monterey. Half an hour later, the nuns knew everything I did about multiverses, Crones, gods—and Drummond's plan to become one—and Rebecca's promise to keep the monastery and its occupants safe from the consortium.

They'd listened without interrupting except for once, when I'd told them about the Mages surrounding the monastery and the gauntlet I'd had to walk, and Sister Colette had pointed an arthritic finger at Methuselah, over whom she'd still hovered.

"*That's* what caused this?" she'd demanded.

"I think so, yes," I'd said. "I don't think he understands that they're on our side."

"*I* don't think I understand that," Sister Lise had muttered.

Sister Bernadette had shushed them both and beckoned me to continue. And now I was done, and so, it seemed, were they. After a long, drawn-out silence, Sister Lise stood and went to the glassware cabinet beside the fridge. She took down four more glasses, cradled two in the crook of one arm with a third in the same hand, and carried the fourth in her other hand back to the table, where she set them down.

Over by Methuselah, Sister Colette picked up the whiskey bottle from the counter beside the sink, tucked it under her arm, and squeaky-wheeled across the kitchen with it, handing it to Sister Bernadette when she arrived tableside. Then she turned the walker around, applied its brakes, and sat on its little bench seat.

In continued silence, Sister Bernadette unscrewed the cap, poured a generous splash of whiskey into each of the new glasses, and topped up my glass before I could object.

Not that I would have tried very hard to stop her.

The nun pushed a glass of whiskey toward each of her colleagues. She cleared her throat. "You're certain you want to take ..." She trailed off and nodded toward the far side of the kitchen.

I let my gaze follow hers, to where Methuselah rocked back and forth in the corner. His toy dragon sat atop his knees, but he ignored it, his shoulders hunched and hands twisted together below his chin as he stared at nothing, his lips moving soundlessly, endlessly repeating a single word.

"*Run,*" they said, and the webs under my skin stirred restlessly.

He might not be shrieking it the way he'd been doing when I'd stepped in from the winter-cloaked courtyard, but it was still damned unnerving.

It was no wonder the poor alien was freaking out, of course. *I* was still unsettled by all the Mages I'd encountered outside the monastery. Rebecca Monterey hadn't been kidding about having more Mages available than had been at the Citadelle, and I had yet to decide if their sheer number was meant to be reassuring or threatening.

But I had to be honest: the idea of taking Methuselah anywhere in this semi-catatonic state made me want to hunch my own shoulders and start rocking, too.

"No," I replied, turning my attention back to Sister Bernadette and her question. I took another mouthful of whiskey—a slightly more generous one this time—and blinked back tears as its burn hit the back of my tongue. I cleared my throat.

"Honestly, I'm not at all certain," I said. "But I don't see much choice. If I leave him here, there's nothing to stop Monterey's collective from breaking their word and grabbing him. Or to stop him from lashing out at them—and maybe you."

Her mouth tightened. Another of *those* looks passed between her and the other nuns, and I scowled. I'd never liked secrets, and I particularly didn't like them under the current circumstances.

"What's going on?" I asked. "What aren't you telling me?"

Sister Simonne slugged back the contents of her glass and set the vessel down with an emphatic *thunk*. She pushed her glasses up on her nose and folded her arms, but for all the determination her pose held, her gaze didn't quite meet mine.

Which made mine narrow.

"The incident with Phoenix that I mentioned ..." she said, letting her words trail off.

The one I'd neglected to follow up on with Phoenix before I said horrible things to her? A thin blade of guilt sliced through my heart.

"What about it?"

Her eyes met mine and danced away again. "He—she—"

"He turned on her when she tried to calm him," Sister Bernadette said. "His hands were … electric, I suppose you'd call them. All he did was point, and—well. I'm sure you saw the burn on her face. We don't think he meant to hurt her, but …"

Shock held both me and my brain immobile as she trailed off, and for long seconds, I couldn't process her words. Words that made no sense, because Methuselah … Phoenix …

Memories of the two of them stirred. Her evolving acceptance of and patience with him; his growing attachment to her and childlike delight in her company; their stand together against the consortium Mages at the Citadelle.

"Can you tell me the princess story again?" I heard his voice ask her. *"The one where the dragon saves her from the mean prince? I like dragons."*

Sister Bernadette's hand clamped around my wrist, and I looked down to find that I'd stood up from my chair.

"Phoenix," I said, by way of explanation.

"Is fine," Sister Simonne assured me. "You saw her, and Sister Lise and I both checked on her upstairs. She just needs …"

"Time," I finished, hoping that the edge of bitterness I heard in my voice would be interpreted as something else. Another look passing between the sisters assured me otherwise, and guilt sliced again. I turned my head toward the door. *I should go to her,* I thought.

"We need to make plans," said Sister Bernadette, tugging gently at my wrist. "And decisions."

"Agreed," Sister Colette said, shoving my glass of whiskey into my hand again as I allowed myself to be drawn back down into my chair. "Starting with Methuselah."

I rested my forearms on the table and hunched over the glass. Staring into the amber liquid, I felt the Ursulines' waiting, their worry—and, in the case of Sister Colette, her impatience—as they waited for me to answer. To lead, when I would have so much rather retreat, preferably into obscurity.

Sweet Mary Magdalene, right about now, I'd have settled for returning to that cocoon on the sidewalk beside the hotel.

Since neither option was—well, an option—and precious seconds were slipping away …

I heaved a sigh, straightened my spine, and said firmly, "I'm taking him with me. I don't trust Rebecca, and if he's slipping that badly, we can't take a chance on him getting away from us. I'm the best one to keep him safe and keep track of him, and to—"

I broke off, unable or unwilling—or both—to voice the possibility that I might have to try to stop Methuselah himself. To turn the stone I was bound to against the very alien who had brought it to Earth.

Would such a thing even be possible? I hoped to hell and back again, twice, that I wouldn't have to find out. So did the Ursulines, judging by the collective sharp inhale around the table.

Sister Bernadette spoke first. "If you're doing this for our sakes, it's not necessary. We knew what we were getting into when we joined the sisterhood, and what the risks were when we agreed to safeguard him."

I *was* doing it for their sakes, but only in part. I also harbored a vague but very real hope that, if push came to shove in Ottawa, Methuselah might yet prove himself useful in helping me take back the stones and find the Weaver. A hope that, if I needed him, he might be a secret weapon of sorts.

An unpredictable and extremely volatile weapon, yes. But, let's face it, if things got to the point where I needed that kind of intervention, we were all going to die anyway. Wisely, I kept that particular thought to myself.

"I'm not *just* doing it for you," I told Sister Bernadette, because we'd come through too much together for me to lie to her. At least not about this. She regarded me through her wire frame glasses, weighing the response. Then she nodded acceptance of my words, choosing not to ask the questions I saw reflected in her eyes.

"Fair enough," she said. "Then we focus on the how. And whether it's wise to take Phoenix with you."

CHAPTER 17

I would leave Phoenix with the Ursulines. The decision was obvious, but it damn near killed me to make it. The thought of not being able to protect her if the Mages came, of choosing Methuselah over her, was almost unbearable.

Worse, however, was the thought of taking her with me and having to make that choice in the heat of the moment, in the middle of a battle; the thought of Methuselah turning on her and having to make that choice; the thought of watching her—

My heart folded in on itself, and my fingers ached in their grip on the whiskey glass. It was all I could do not to pitch it across the room in fury and guilt and agony and—

And fuck, because I didn't even know *what* I felt, because not all of what seethed through me belonged to me. Some of it was the darkness, some of it was the stone. All of it was too big for words.

I drained my glass and coughed at the fire sliding down my throat and into my chest. Sister Bernadette quietly poured another two fingers' worth. Again, I didn't demur. Again, I drained it—and hoped to hell as I did (and fuzziness claimed my toes) that the Mages wouldn't choose now to attack.

Or maybe that they will, and we can just be done with this whole fucking mess, a belligerent voice muttered in my head.

Oof.

But it had a point.

But *oof.*

I put my hand over the glass and shook my head as Sister Bernadette held the bottle aloft in query. Me and my voices had all had quite enough.

Sister Bernadette set the whiskey aside. "Right," she said briskly. "We need a travel plan for two of you."

"It has to be via land," Sister Lise said. "Our contingency fund would cover the airfare, but Methuselah doesn't have ID, and Sister Monica …?"

She looked over her glasses at me, and I shook my head in answer to the unfinished question, because I'd been a non-person since Toronto. Before that, actually, given that all of my identification had been lost in the house I'd shared with the nuns of St. Mary's before—

Well. Before.

"Not the train, either," I said, shuddering at the memories of a destroyed train car, a half-wrecked bridge, and watching a Mage drown in front of me. "At least, not unless it's the only option we have."

"Train travel would be too complicated," Sister Lise said. "The bridge hasn't reopened yet, and we'd have to route you through Saguenay. It would be too long a long trip for—" She tipped her head toward Methuselah.

"Agreed," Sister Colette said, shifting her weight on her walker seat. "Which leaves us with what? Lending them St. Christopher?"

Sister Simonne, the designated driver among the Ursulines, snorted at the idea of letting me use the monastery's ancient station wagon that had been named—optimistically, I thought, after having ridden in it—after the patron saint of travelers. Although I couldn't say much, given that I'd once driven an almost-identical vehicle named St. Jude after the patron saint of lost causes.

"I love that car to death," the nun was saying, "and he's great for around the city, but his top speed is what, fifty kilometers an hour? At highway speeds, he'd fall apart before the other side of the river. Besides, Sister Monica has no ID, remember? That means no driver's license, either."

Sister Colette nodded agreement, and the three of them

subsided into thoughtful silence as they mulled over the travel problem. I tried to mull, too, but after lunch with Rebecca followed by running the Mage corridor home and then the Phoenix thing and *way* too much whiskey, there wasn't much left in the way of viable synapses in my brain.

The thought of Phoenix made me briefly consider going in search of her, but my lack of synapses vetoed that idea, too. We'd either get in another fight or I'd cry all over her, and she didn't need either of those things from me.

My restless gaze landed on the alien in the corner, and my heart contracted. Poor Methuselah. Of all of us, he was probably most in need of comfort and reassurance. The last of his kind except for the dying Weaver, hunted by the consortium, losing a little more of his mind every day …

And now I was going to drag him away from everything familiar, including the young woman he'd bonded with. Not-entirely-sober tears filled my eyes at the idea of his confusion and loneliness. I blinked them away before anyone noticed and pushed back from the table. Leaving the nuns immersed in a discussion I was too tired to take part in, I went to join the alien in the corner.

His rocking had slowed but not stopped, and he was still mouthing the word *run* as I settled myself on the floor beside him, but he didn't pull away when I took one of his hands in mine.

I slipped the stone into my pocket—freaking hell, the way I kept finding it in my hand, I was surprised it hadn't taken root there—and cupped his long, wrinkled fingers between my own. The effects of the whiskey seemed to have tapered off with my brief tearfulness, more was the pity. I'd never been drunk before, and today seemed as fine a time as any to give it a whirl. To forget, just for a little while. Or at least not to care so much.

I bumped my shoulder gently against Methuselah's. "I

know there are Mages out there," I whispered to him, "but it's all right. They're protecting us from the others."

He rocked faster again. Remembering the way the webs had crawled along my skin as I'd walked the gauntlet along the monastery's street, I didn't blame him.

"It's all right for now," I amended. "They don't want you, Methuselah, and they don't want our stone." *Yet.*

"Run," he muttered. "Run."

"We're going to," I said. "You and me. We're going to run together. But we can't run forever, Methuselah. We have to stop them. We have to stop the Mages. Do you understand?"

"Run," he said.

Frustration rippled through me, tugging on the stone's webs beneath my skin—and on those that crisscrossed the surface of my palms. Methuselah abruptly stopped moving and stared down at the hand that was sandwiched between mine. The child-eyes lifted to meet my gaze.

"You're feeding it too much," he observed.

Fine ice crystals filtered through my belly. "How—how do you know?"

He turned one of my palms up and pointed at the film of spiderweb covering it. "You're disappearing."

I shook my head. "No, that's only because I got hurt," I said. "I was burned, and the webs are helping until I heal."

The child's eyes turned sad. "You're disappearing," he repeated.

The ice in my belly spread through my veins, and I fought not to drop his hand. Or to shove it away from me. I swallowed hard. "Okay," I said. "How do I stop it?"

"Run," he said cheerfully. Then he took his hand from mine, picked up the dragon from his knee, and vaulted to his feet. Leaving me on the floor, he flew the toy across the kitchen and out the door. His roars followed him, dying away as the door swung shut behind him.

My heart lurched. *Phoenix,* I thought as the incident the

nuns had described loomed in my brain. I scrambled to my feet, then clutched for the corner of the counter when my knees gave an unexpected wobble. Perhaps the whiskey had done a tad more than make me tearful after all.

But it still hadn't erased the caring.

Before I could thrust myself away from the counter to stagger after Methuselah, however, Sister Bernadette rose to my rescue—and from her chair at the table.

"Sister Simonne will go," she said, swaying her way toward me. "I'm sure everything is fine now that he's calmed down, but she'll call if she needs help, won't you, Sister Simonne?"

"Of course." The solid form of Sister Simonne was already on its way to the door. It was swaying, too. Or—

Oh, hell. That was me doing the swaying and not them, wasn't it?

Sister Bernadette's face loomed large in front of mine, and I gave a little yelp of surprise. Then a hiccup. Sister Bernadette frowned at me.

"Are you all right?" she asked. "You look like you might faint."

I was pretty sure the correct phrase was *pass out*, but I kept the thought to myself and—despite the decided and undeniable wooziness that had set in—nodded. It was my automatic response to others' concerns about me, developed and honed over a lifetime, because I had always been the strong one and not the other way around. A verbal reassurance of *"I'm fine"* usually followed the nod, but this time, as it hovered on the tip of my tongue, I hesitated, caught off guard by a feeling of uncertainty. Vulnerability.

I blamed the whiskey.

And the stone.

The latter had found its way into my hand again. Its edges dug into my fingers and palm, and its webs shifted and rippled through my body, some like gossamer, others—the ones that held me together in far too many places—like threads of steel. All reminders that I was far, far from fine anymore.

A slow shake of my head replaced the nod.

"No," I said, pitching my voice low so the others didn't hear. I met the nun's gray eyes, seeing only calm reflected in their surface, but knowing that worry lurked beneath. I hesitated, reluctant to add to the latter when she already had so much to deal with. But Sister Bernadette would want me to tell her, just as I would her, if our roles were reversed.

"The darkness—the stone—" I broke off, gripped the object of my not-inconsiderable distress harder, and summoned every atom of willpower I possessed in order to speak aloud the deep, dark fear that had been plaguing me. The one that had been taking over my thoughts, my breath, and my heart ... quite literally.

I took a deep breath and told her about my collapse on the sidewalk and my lost hours, and how I'd lashed out at Phoenix, finishing in a quiet voice, "It's changing me, sister. The stone, I mean. It's changing me, and I don't think I can do this. I don't think I'm strong enough. I think the darkness is winning."

The nun didn't answer at first, instead turning her head to watch the others. Sister Colette remained at the table; Sister Lise had moved to the counter and was spooning instant coffee into a mug. The whiskey and I suspected it was meant for us.

My thoughts drifted out of the kitchen, wondering how Phoenix was. If Methuselah had found her. If they were okay together again. If she and I would ever be okay together again. I knew Sister Simonne would look after her for now, but sooner or later, I was going to have to speak to her about what I'd said, about what she expected, about Talia ...

About me leaving and her staying.

More tears prickled behind my eyes. I didn't know if I could do that, either.

"You can, you know," Sister Bernadette said.

I blinked, taken aback by her sudden mind-reading ability. "Pardon?"

The gray gaze returned to mine. "You can find the stones. You can take them from the consortium. You can help save the Weaver. And you can absolutely hold back the darkness."

Oh. That. I sniffled against the tears. Damned whiskey. Then I shook my head.

"But I—"

She didn't let me finish. "Belief is a powerful thing, Sister Monica," she said. "It's like prayer that way, especially when it's shared by many. *You* might not believe in yourself, but we do. We do, and Talia does, and all the sisters who helped get you this far do. Even Methuselah believes you can save the Weaver, and that—that belief is a little like intention when it comes to magick. The kind of intention that will carry you through, if you trust it."

She meant well. I knew that. And I knew she believed—no pun intended—what she said. But sweet Mary Magdalene, her words sounded more like a sentence being handed down than they did encouragement, settling like a thick, heavy hangman's noose around my neck. Their weight made my knees buckle, and it took everything in me to remain upright. To look her in the eye. To attempt a smile in return as I thought about the monumental task facing me. The many monumental tasks.

First, I would have to hold my darkness at bay while I somehow got myself and Methuselah to Ottawa, then I'd have to find a way to get us into the Global Economic Forum and past who-knew-how-many Mages so I could steal the stones, then I'd need a way to get us *and* the stones *out* of the forum, and then—

Hell, I couldn't think further than that, because all of *that* was already impossible enough. The rest of it—the saving-the-Weaver part?

A wave of self-pity washed over me, and I let it pull me under, because knowing what I'd learned about gods and goddesses and portals and multiverses, the saving-the-Weaver part really was too much. Really was impossible. Really was—

Without warning, the stone turned to fire in my grasp. So hot and so fast that I instinctively opened my hand and tried to fling it away. It didn't let me, of course, and as fast as it had heated, it cooled again—as if in breaking my downward spiral, it had done what it set out to do. That, and it had reminded me that I wasn't alone. Not in any of this, because I had it. I always had it, whether I liked it or not.

"Sister Monica?" Sister Bernadette prompted me. "Did you hear what I said?"

I looked up from the stone to meet her eyes. A noncommittal agreement formed on my tongue, then died there as her words really did sink in. *You might not believe in yourself, but we do. We do, and Talia does, and all the sisters who helped get you this far do.*

All the sisters …

My gaze shifted past Sister Bernadette's shoulder to where Sister Lise poured water from the kettle into the mug of instant coffee. From there, it went to Sister Colette, who had moved from her walker to a chair and was trying to pretend she wasn't watching me, although the pinch of concern between her brows gave her away, and then to Sister Simonne, returning just then through the doorway into the kitchen.

I lingered for a moment on her face but saw no worry there, which meant that Methuselah and Phoenix were both safe. A tiny part of me felt a tiny bit better. The rest of me stepped back to stare at the big picture coming into focus.

I began with Methuselah, the man-child-alien who had started all this but then sacrificed a thousand lifetimes to try to repair it, bringing the stones across who knew how many universes and then holding onto his drifting faculties long enough to pass on his story—and his responsibility.

Then I thought about all that everyone in our little group

had done to get us as far as we'd come. About Talia, who absolutely wouldn't want me to come for her and who would understand when I didn't; about Phoenix, who had survived against so many odds in so many ways but had never once wavered in her determination—or her loyalty to me. About the sisterhood that had formed to protect Methuselah and his stones for millennia; the nuns who had given their lives to save mine in Toronto; the women who had helped keep us hidden in Kingston; the nuns who had gone to battle for me here and would without doubt find a way to get me to Ottawa.

I thought about them all and found myself mildly astonished at how very much *not* alone I was—or had been—in any of this. I just hadn't stopped moving long enough to realize it.

The nun beside me cupped my chin in her hand and turned my head until my gaze met hers. "Belief," she reiterated in a quiet voice, "is intentional."

I sincerely hoped she was right.

I brushed at a tickle on my cheek, surprised—but not really—to find tears there. I swiped them away, swept one last glance over the kitchen and its occupants, and then leaned forward to Sister Bernadette's cheek. Or perhaps it was the whiskey that did that, but whatever.

"Thank you," I told the nun, because right or wrong, she had done her best to give me hope, and for that she deserved my gratitude. For that, and for so much more, including the reminder that mending bridges needed to be intentional, too.

Chapter 18

I found Phoenix in one of the rocking chairs in the living room, her knees drawn up against her chest in classic Phoenix fashion as she stared into the flames in the little wood stove. Methuselah was there, too, sitting quietly on the floor over by the bookcase that hid the nuns' stash of Molotov cocktails. He was flipping through the pages of a children's picture book and showing the illustrations to his dragon, and I leaned a shoulder against the doorframe, my misgivings returning as I watched him.

How, I thought bleakly, would I ever get him all the way to Ottawa with me? Or into the heart of the consortium to steal the remaining stones? Or—assuming I survived long enough—beyond that, to wherever the Weaver was?

"Belief," whispered Sister Bernadette, *"is intentional."*

And what about blind faith, I wondered. Did that count, too? Because I was pretty sure that where Methuselah was concerned, it was all I had. Or sheer stubbornness on my part. Take your pick.

I snorted softly, and Phoenix looked over at the sound. She contemplated me for a moment, then waggled the fingers of one hand at me. Deciding to interpret it as an invitation, I detached my shoulder from the doorframe and walked over to join her.

She spoke first. "I'm sorry," she said as I settled into the rocking chair beside her.

"You're sorry? For what? I'm the one who owes you an apology," I replied. "The way I spoke to you ..." I trailed off, my insides cringing at the memory of my voice, my words, my unforgivable harshness.

But Phoenix was shaking her head. "You had a right to be

angry. I was—can be—*am* selfish sometimes, and I wasn't thinking. I know we can't just go after Talia, and I understand why. And Sister Simonne and I talked, and—"

She broke off and took a deep breath, returning her gaze to the fire, then finished in a rush, "And I know I can't go with you and Methuselah, and it's okay. I promise. I'll be fine here with the sisters. Just—just make sure you come home again, okay?"

I rocked gently for a moment, staring into the flames. "That's it?" I asked finally. "You don't want to hear the carefully rehearsed groveling I planned to deliver?"

The corner of her mouth twitched in my peripheral vision. "I mean, if you really want to," she said, "then I won't stop you. But honestly, I get why you were ..."

"So nasty?" I suggested.

Her hands, resting atop her bent knees as she picked at her cuticles, went still. She didn't answer. I reached out with my empty hand and laid it, palm up, on the arm of her rocker.

"I *was* angry, Phoenix," I said, "but that was no excuse for how I spoke to you. You didn't deserve that, and I'm sorry."

She stared at my upturned hand, then sighed and placed one of her own in it. "I know," she said simply, and just like that, we were okay again.

THE FOUR URSULINES SPENT THE NEXT TWELVE HOURS chasing down leads in the Obsidian Sisterhood and trying to coordinate a way for me to get to Ottawa. The lack of connection within the sisterhood—once a critical part of keeping Methuselah's and the stones' whereabouts safe—was an enormous liability when communication was needed.

Sisters Bernadette, Lise, and Simonne took turns working

through the night to make calls, one after another after another, to all corners of the world. Not because we expected someone in Greece to be able to give us a lift, but because someone in the little seaside village of Petalidi there might know someone in Reykjavik, Iceland, who might in turn know someone in Sydney, Australia, who …

Well. That had been the hope, anyway. But the next morning, a weary Sister Bernadette made her way into the dining room, the last to join the table for breakfast, and sagged into her chair.

"I've tried everyone," she said, pushing her glasses up on her head and rubbing her eyes. "We Ursulines are the only ones left of the Obsidians in Quebec that anyone knows of, and any leads we were given between here and Ottawa turned out to be …" She trailed off, and the other nuns exchanged knowing looks and nods of understanding.

"What?" Phoenix asked from beside Sister Simonne, and then, as understanding dawned on her, too, she sat back in her chair and hunched her shoulders. "Oh. All of them?"

"Our numbers have been diminishing for many years," Sister Lise told her. "Today's young women are unwilling to give up their …"

She, too, trailed off, and Phoenix looked between her, the other Ursulines, and me. "Their …?" she prompted us in general.

Sister Colette snorted. "Their witchy side," she said bluntly. "Once, the pendulum swung away from magick and women forgot what they were; now it is swinging the other way—too far so for the sisterhood's purposes. Did that Margaret person not tell you any of this?"

That Margaret person referring to the nun who had first given me the stone and whose ultimate betrayal had led to the Citadelle battle and the taking of Talia. Her name sounded foreign, now, and I didn't think I'd heard it spoken since that night. I certainly hadn't uttered it myself, because as far as traitors went, Margaret had been the worst kind.

I dragged myself back to the present as Phoenix looked at me in inquiry, both her eyebrows disappearing under her bright pink bangs. "Um … did she?" she asked.

I shook my head. "She didn't explain it like that, no. She just said that we were all witches—or had the potential to be—but to be an Obsidian sister, you had to renounce your magick."

"But why?"

Sister Simonne laid a gentle hand on her arm. "Think about what they've done to witches, dear heart. And how hard they sought them."

"Oh," said Phoenix again. Then, as the deaths of hundreds of thousands of women over the centuries settled into her, she repeated, "*Oh*. I never thought … wait. So all of you—" She gestured at the nuns with her free hand, leaving her other arm under Sister Simonne's touch. "All of you were *witches*?"

Sister Bernadette smiled a tired smile. "All of us *could* have been witches," she agreed. "But remember that there is more than one way to raise magick, especially when you're with a like-minded group."

Heads bobbed around the table, and Phoenix looked to me for clarification again.

"Think about lauds," I said, reminding her of the time she'd joined the nuns for their morning prayers before deciding it was just too early for her. *"Intense,"* she'd called it. *"There's an energy when they pray together."*

"But—wasn't that just prayer?"

"And what is prayer but the setting of intention?" Sister Bernadette reached for the coffee carafe. "Just as magick is."

Her gaze lifted from her cup to meet mine for an instant. *Just as belief is*, it reminded me.

I still hoped blind faith qualified, too.

"I never thought of it that way," Phoenix said.

"Few do anymore," said Sister Lise with a sigh. She slid a plate of cold French toast across to Sister Bernadette. "Why do you think we're all so old here? Although, to be fair, there is a great deal more freedom in the life of a witch than there is in the life of a nun."

"But I thought that not all of the Obsidian Sisterhood were nuns."

"They're not. Our sisterhood spans the entire globe, and its history predates even the church. Most are still women of religion, however, because what better place to hide from the ones who sought us—who sought the stones and Methuselah—than within the ranks of the seekers?"

Phoenix stared at her. Then at each of the others. Then she shook her head, but in wonder rather than disagreement, and muttered, "Holy shit. Pardon my French, but it's no wonder you guys have kept everything hidden for as long as you have. You're downright devious."

I expected the Ursulines to brush off the somewhat backhanded praise, but instead, they exchanged glances, then tiny grins.

"We are, aren't we?" Sister Lise mused.

"We should get T-shirts when this is over," Sister Colette added. "The Obsidian Sisterhood, Saving Your Asses Since 4100 B.C."

"Give or take a few hundred years," said Sister Simonne, as if accuracy of that degree mattered.

Sister Colette rolled her eyes at her colleague, and then the tiny grins around the table faded, and the lighter moment passed as if someone had flicked a get-back-to-business switch. Sister Bernadette swallowed the bite of French toast she'd taken and cleared her throat.

"We need new ideas," she said. "If the sisterhood can't help, then—"

"Louis," Sister Colette interrupted with a smack of her

hand on the table, apropos of nothing but sounding triumphant.

All heads swiveled toward her. Sister Colette regarded each of her colleagues through her thick glasses, rolled her eyes, and transferred her owl-like gaze to me.

"*Louis*," she repeated, enunciating the syllables in a slow, exaggerated fashion. She smacked the table again impatiently when the blank looks continued. "You know. The truck driver."

"You mean Louis O'Connor?" Sister Simonne asked. "The man who drove us to the Citadelle that night?"

"Do we know another Louis-the-truck-driver?" Sister Colette demanded with another eyeball roll. "Think about it. If he's not going to Ottawa himself, he might know someone who is."

"Huh," said Sister Lise as I processed the *O'Connor* part of Louis-the-truck-driver's name. I'd had no idea he was one of the *Québécois* descended from Irish ancestors—our introductions when he'd rescued me roadside by the trainyard that night hadn't been that formal.

"Sister Colette might have something there," Sister Lise continued. "If anyone can get Sister Monica a ride, a trucker can. They talk to one another on those radios of theirs all the time. I saw it in a movie once."

I swallowed a snort and opened my mouth to object, but Sister Bernadette beat me to it.

"It's too risky," she said, shaking her head. "If the Mages happen to come after Sister Monica, the driver could get hurt —or worse. We can't ask that of someone who isn't in the sisterhood."

Sister Colette huffed. "You've come up with another idea, then?"

"Well, no, but—"

"Then I vote we ask Louis and let him—or whoever he puts us in touch with—decide."

Sister Bernadette's head continued to shake, but it lacked conviction. I intervened hastily, before she caved to the idea.

"Sister Bernadette is right," I said, pushing away the half-eaten breakfast I'd lost all appetite for. "The risk is too great. Even if I had a way to contact him, and I don't, I can't put him—or anyone—in that kind of danger. We have to find—"

"*That* kind of danger?" Sister Colette interrupted. "What about the kind where the Mages figure out the stones, and this darkness you've told us about unmakes the Weaver and him and all the rest of us?"

Well. When she put it like that ...

I snapped my teeth shut and met Sister Bernadette's gaze, reading the same capitulation in her expression that I felt in myself, along with a grimness that sent a sliver of ice into my very core. None of this was going to go well, I thought. None of it at all.

And we had no alternative.

The head of the Ursulines pushed away from the table and stood.

"He gave me his contact information the night he helped us," she said. "I have it upstairs in my office. I'll call him now."

CHAPTER 19

Louis-the-truck-driver, bless his heart, didn't hesitate.

I'd accompanied Sister Bernadette up to her office while she called him, pacing the bookshelf-lined room that so poignantly reminded me of Sister Ernestine's office in my former lifetime. While I caught only a handful of words in the one-sided, rapid-fire French conversation, I could tell the direction it was taking from the gratitude and relief in the nun's voice. She pulled a pad of paper and pen from her desk drawer and jotted down notes as she listened and asked questions, and I stopped at the window to hold the lace curtain aside and look down on the quiet winter street.

A Mage was there, huddled into a puffy down parka on the corner as he leaned against a lamp post. Even if he hadn't been staring up at the exact window in which I stood, as if he sensed my presence there, the twitch of the spiderwebs running through me would have given him away. I held his challenging gaze without blinking, caught up in a silent confrontation from which I refused to back down. It was what Lissa had called a pissing contest back in the days of the Mary Magdalene House for Women.

When things had been simpler. Less earth- and universe-devouring.

When good memories such as Lissa hadn't slid like a stiletto between my ribs and into my heart.

It took every ounce of willpower I possessed to maintain my stare, but after a few moments, the Mage's lips twisted into the semblance of a smile, and he inclined his head and turned away.

For what it was worth, I'd won our standoff. Word was definitely getting around about what I could do to a Mage.

The idea didn't reassure me, however. Rather, it sent a shiver of foreboding down my spine, because what one Mage might be afraid of, many working together would still try to challenge, and then—

The stone stirred in my grasp. Closing my eyes, I let the curtain drop and clutched the window frame to steady myself against a sway. Against the memories of that night at the Citadelle, when I'd come so very close to losing myself.

In my mind's eye, I watched again as silver strands writhed outward, away from the stone—from me—and across the pavement to wrap around a Mage whose fingers danced in the summoning of his magick. I heard him cry out as the webs wrapped around his ankles and began to encase his legs, listened to his scream as they climbed his body and forced themselves beneath his skin, felt the heat from my core turn to a fire that blasted outward from me and engulfed him.

A heat that had writhed through me and around me and *in* me until I wanted to shriek as the Mage had done. Remembered panic filled my chest and clogged my throat. I had so nearly lost myself to it that night, I thought. The stone had turned on me as it had done to the others that it had bound with before me, and it had almost devoured my darkness. Devoured me. I shuddered.

And the Mages thought *they* were afraid? *Hah*.

"*Bon*," said Sister Bernadette crisply, as she replaced the handset of the monastery's landline phone.

Welcoming the interruption—because holy Mother, I could do without *any* of those memories—I turned to her, crossing my arms and leaning a shoulder against the bookcase beside the window. The stone remained in my hand.

"I take it he agreed to help?" I asked.

It both did and didn't surprise me, given what he'd seen when he'd driven the sisters to the Citadelle that night, arriving in the nick of time to distract the Mages enough to turn the tables in my favor.

Louis-the-truck-driver hadn't so much as hesitated, not even when faced with the goliath, the Mages' monster. He was cut from a special kind of cloth, my roadside knight.

"He's committed to a run up to Saguenay himself, but he thinks his *tante* Lucille might be hauling a load to Ottawa tomorrow. He's going to check with her and—"

"Tante?"

"His aunt."

In spite of the bookcase's support, I almost fell over. "His *aunt* drives long haul?"

"They own the trucking company, together with Louis's sister," Sister Bernadette said. Then she pursed her lips and looked down her nose at me. "Or were you questioning her ability to drive a truck at her age?"

"Of course not," I denied quickly, shaking my head in an absolute lie, because given that Louis himself was in his mid- to late-seventies, the idea that his even older aunt might be beyond her driving prime was exactly the first thought that had sprung to mind. "I'm just surprised that a woman of her —*our*—generation had the opportunity to become a truck driver, that's all."

My cobbled-together excuse sounded lame to my own ears, especially when Sister Bernadette let it sit between us for several long seconds without comment before taking pity on me and letting it slide.

"Yes," she said at last. "Well. As I was saying, Louis said he would call Lucille and ask her to get in touch with us if she—"

The phone on the desk rang, and the nun reached to answer it. "*Oui*," she responded to a caller I couldn't hear, and then she nodded and turned away, dropping into rapid-fire French, none of which I understood beyond a repeat of *oui*, followed by a name as she said her farewells.

Lucille.

Methuselah and I had our ride to Ottawa.

CHAPTER 20

We left at three the next morning.

There was no way to drive an eighteen-wheeler into the walled portion of the city that was Old Quebec, and so we'd arranged to meet Louis's aunt along the river beside Lower Town at three thirty. The walk was only about fifteen minutes, Sister Bernadette had assured me, but I'd doubled that for my own peace of mind. Between icy streets and unpredictable aliens, I wasn't ruling out delays.

And so, mittened, hatted, and otherwise armored against the bitter wind and cold waiting for us outside the monastery's front door, I turned to find him—immune to the weather himself—waiting with his usual trench coat on and fedora in place. Phoenix stood next to him, her hands shoved into her hoodie pockets, flanked by the four Ursulines.

My world stood still.

This was it. I was really doing it. I was leaving her behind. Just her, with no Talia to look out for her, and no guarantee that I would return. It would be her and four elderly women whose remaining days on Earth, even if they all survived this, were limited, and then what? What would my girl do then?

She had no ID, no job, no money of her own … she wasn't even a resident of the province we'd landed in. What would she do when her hormone pills ran out? Or if she was injured? Or—

"You're doing it again," said Phoenix.

My thoughts skidded to a halt. She was right. We'd been up until well past ten the night before going over these exact same scenarios—and other disasters like them—instead of me getting the sleep I was so desperately going to need. And she'd had the same response for each of them: *You worry too much.*

Which, yes, valid, but—

I opened my mouth to remind her of all the reasons I had *to* worry, but she placed a gentle finger across my lips, cutting me off before I'd uttered a sound. I blinked my surprise at her —not just at the gesture, but at the steady calm behind it.

"I'm okay with this," she said. "Truly. I can't help you get the stones, and I'll just be in the way. You have enough to worry about"—she sent a speaking glance over my shoulder to where Methuselah waited—"without me to look after, too."

I hesitated, then, because I couldn't help myself from going over at least one of the disaster scenarios—especially this one—I burst out, "But what if the consortium—"

"Hah!" Sister Colette piped up. "Let them try. By tomorrow, the Molotovs will be fully restocked. The Mages won't know what hit them."

I scowled, first because of the interruption, and second, because *that* was supposed to make me feel better?

"I want to stay," Phoenix continued. "I want to help protect the monastery so that you and Talia and Methuselah have somewhere to come back to."

On the verge of further argument, I hesitated. I hated the idea of leaving her behind with the Ursulines, but was it really any more dangerous than bringing her with me? At least here, she'd have—for what it was worth—Rebecca's Mages watching over the monastery while she waited for us. And, I thought as my mouth twisted, she'd have the nuns—for a while, anyway—if none of us made it back.

Because let's face it, the likelihood that we would was ... slim.

Talia's return depended on me fulfilling a tenuous agreement with Rebecca Monterey—whom I didn't trust as far as I could throw despite her *"my word is my bond"* bullshit, because Mages. My own continued existence was very much up in the air, because Mages, remaining stones, more Mages, and likely a monster or two. And Methuselah, whom I didn't dare leave behind (because, again, Mages) was—

Well.

I had no idea what would become of him once we had the stones … if we got them.

No idea at all.

"You're right," I said. I swallowed against the gruffness in my voice. "You'll be as safe here as you would be with me. Maybe more so."

I hoped.

But, let's face it, it was a proverbial crap shoot either way.

"Plus," she said. "I can keep looking for Talia, and if you need me to, I can help track Drummond. You know, in case Rebecca was wrong about the Ottawa thing."

Dear sweet Mary, I hoped not. I wasn't sure I had it in me for a second travel-planning session if I had to go elsewhere.

"That reminds me," Phoenix continued. "Do you have enough money for a burner phone if you need one? Actually, you *will* need one so that you can call us when it's—when you're—"

"Sister Bernadette gave me some money," I assured her. "For incidentals and the like. I'm sure there's enough to cover a phone when I need one."

The blue eyes clouded with what I was pretty sure were the same memories of Toronto that were going through my own head. The ones from back at the beginning of our journey, before we understood what was happening, or knew about Mages and the many minions they had spread throughout places like police forces who could track vehicles and bank cards and—

Phoenix cleared her throat. "Good. Just don't activate it until you need it. You know, in case."

"I won't," I promised. Like her, I didn't want another store clerk dying because of a fleeting association with me. Although that was unlikely now. The Mages didn't need to trace my movements anymore. Not now that they knew where to find the people I most cared about. "But I'll call as soon as —well. You know."

She gave me a watery half-grin, half-grimace, then nodded past me to where Methuselah waited by the door. "You'll look after him for me?"

I followed her gaze and nodded, too. "I will," I promised. Then I looked back at her. "And you'll look after you?"

The tears clinging to her lashes spilled over onto her cheeks. She sniffled a little and swiped a sleeve over first one cheek, then the other, then the first again before squaring her shoulders firmly.

"I will. I'll have lots to keep me occupied and out of the nuns' hair, what with looking for the—" She stopped, and her gaze slid away.

I frowned. "With the what?"

"Oh"—she flapped her tear-dampened arm in a vague gesture—"you know. Computer stuff. I'm … helping Sister Bernadette."

My frown deepened at the oddly hesitant response, but before I could pursue it, Sister Colette nudged her walker against my boot-clad ankle.

"Your ride won't wait forever," she said, "and we're not likely to find another if you miss it. Not in time."

Her warning was dire, but it wasn't wrong. Abandoning the distraction of Phoenix's odd response, I turned my attention back to the looming task before me and pulled my again-tearful Phoenix in for a final hug.

"Be careful," I whispered. "And always remember that I love you."

I released her quickly, before I could rethink—again—the decision to leave her behind. Amid a last flurry of goodbyes and stay-safes from the nuns, Methuselah and I slipped away from the cozy, familiar warmth of the monastery and into the dark winter night …

Where the gauntlet waited.

CHAPTER 21

I didn't know how Methuselah would react to leaving the monastery.

He'd left of his own accord before, of course, and had been gone for months, but that had been before Phoenix and I had arrived—and before she'd tried to protect him from the Mages on the night of the Citadelle. He'd become increasingly close to her since then, and while I felt sure he'd be okay without the nuns, I wasn't as certain about him leaving the young woman.

Or about how I was going to get him past the Mages who watched that leaving.

As we walked down the center of the dark street, *tense* didn't begin to describe my shoulders. Or my spine. Or my jaw.

And it certainly didn't begin to describe the hand that clutched the stone.

From the instant we'd emerged from the monastery complex's courtyard, every gaze had been on us, the way they'd been on me when I'd returned from meeting Rebecca. Only this time, I had Methuselah to worry about. Would they come after him, now that he was out in the open? Would the consortium launch an attack, because they'd been watching after all?

I told myself that my imagination was working overtime. I felt reasonably certain that Rebecca had told the truth, and she really *didn't* want to destroy the universe the way Drummond did—at least, not for the moment. Besides, if her Mages had wanted to grab Methuselah outright, four stone walls wouldn't have stopped them.

As for the consortium, they already had their plan in place

—one that they had no reason to believe had already gone awry. They wanted Methuselah *and* me, and they were arrogant in their confidence that I would hand us over when they were ready.

And so, I squared my shoulders, lifted my chin, and—with the stone in my hand and Methuselah beside me—started down the road. Past the parked cars, past the curtains lifted away from windows, past the hostile, calculating gazes.

Methuselah's step had hitched once, when the monastery door had closed behind us, and I had braced for the worst—not knowing what that would even look like. But he'd merely closed his hand around his dragon toy, tucked it safely into his pocket, and begun trudging across the snowy cobblestones without comment or fuss.

Once we were clear of the Mage gauntlet, the streets turned deserted, with no one and nothing up and about but us. Our footsteps thudded dully over packed snow and ice in some places and bare pavement in others, their muffled echoes bouncing back to us from the stone buildings lining our way.

My imagination continued to work overtime, raising the hairs on the back of my neck with its certainty that we were being followed, despite repeated glances over my shoulder assuring me otherwise. Not until we reached the first landing on the wooden steps leading down to Lower Town did either of us speak, and then, simultaneously, we both did.

"Methuselah," I began, "I'm not sure—"

"I can find them," he said.

I stopped—both walking and talking—to stare at him. Okay, that statement definitely won out over anything I'd been going to say about what we might expect from Louis's aunt, or my concerns about how she would react to Methuselah's shifts from man to child and back again.

I tucked my mittened hands into my pockets and turned my back to the wind coming in from the river below, hunching my shoulders against the bitter cold it carried. We stood beneath a lamp post, but Methuselah's fedora shaded his face from the light, and I couldn't see his eyes—or look for the galaxies there to know whether this was one of his all-there moments.

"The stones, you mean?" I asked.

"Yes." The fedora-ed head nodded slowly. "I can feel them when they're near. They want me to come to them. That was one of the reasons the sisterhood sent them away from me."

No one had mentioned such a reason to me, but I doubted it was a deliberate omission. It was more likely that no one knew anymore, that it was just one more thing that had been lost in the Obsidian Sisterhood's deliberate lack of record-keeping—or sharing.

"I can feel them at a distance, too," he murmured, turning his head to gaze out across the river, "but it's not as strong. Most of the time, I can ignore them." His shoulders drooped. "I never told them that. The sisters, I mean, or any of my keepers before them."

I opened my mouth to respond, then closed it again, because I had no idea what to say. I studied him as if seeing him for the first time. Which I was, in a sense.

I realized with a sudden pang that I'd been so caught up in finding him, then protecting him, then digging information out of him in his lucid moments, that I'd never stopped to wonder about *him*. About—

Well, about the alien behind the alien, I supposed.

I'd never thought about how he had indeed been *kept* by the sisterhood for millennia, or considered how he'd felt about that, or how he might feel now about me dragging him off in pursuit of—

"You worry too much about others," he said, interrupting my flow of revelations and throwing me off stride a second time.

I blinked up at him from beneath the toque that had slid down my forehead to rest over my eyebrows. "Pardon?"

"And you overthink."

"I—"

"You won't have time for either of those when we get to the stones," he interrupted. "You'll need to be quick. Decisive. You weren't responsible for all the things that happened before this, but now you are. You have no choice."

I was still processing the vulnerable side of him that I'd glimpsed, and his switch to suddenly matter-of-fact—also new —caught me off guard. My mouth dropped open, but before I could gather my wits enough to respond, he continued.

"I don't have long like this," he said, gesturing at himself. "My mind is … hard to access sometimes. So, please, just listen."

His mind was hard to access *sometimes*? I shoved the thought aside—along with my shock and the nagging reminders from my brain about Louis's aunt waiting for us— and nodded agreement. I didn't need to see Methuselah's eyes to know that the galaxies had returned to them.

"The stones want to be a box again," he said, "but I cannot remake them. The darkness they seek to contain is in me, too, perhaps more so than it is in any of the Mages. Whatever happens, you must keep them away from me. I cannot be trusted with them, do you understand?"

More darkness in him than in any of the Mages? Holy hell, I hoped not.

"I—but how?" I asked.

"*Listen*," he snarled. "There are three things I have to tell you while I still can."

I took a tiny, startled step back, because nope, I hadn't seen this facet of him before, either. Was it what had surfaced when he attacked Phoenix? A chill that had nothing to do with the bitter January wind seeped through me, and I buried my face in the scarf wrapped around my neck, both to stay warm and as a reminder to myself to keep my mouth shut.

"First, you must keep the stones away from me," he reiterated, "and second, you must not, under any circumstances, touch them yourself."

That was a given. I pressed my lips together to keep from saying so and nodded again. Then I waited as Methuselah stared again across Lower Town and the river below.

And waited.

And—

"Third," he said finally, heavily, "you must promise me the impossible. If you succeed, if you find the stones and take them from the Mages, you must promise you will find Grandmother Weaver and save her."

Wait—what?

My chin popped up out of the scarf, and I gaped at him. "Without you, you mean? But I thought—"

"Monica," he said.

I stopped talking out of sheer surprise at hearing my name on his lips. In all the weeks I'd known him, it was the first time he'd ever spoken it.

He stared over my head toward the river, silent for so long that I thought I might have lost him again, but then he sighed and looked down at me again. "I cannot go with you to find her," he said. "I am … fading … too fast. There won't be enough of me left to help you, and whatever is left"—he lifted his shoulders in a slow shrug—"whatever is left will only hinder you. You must go alone."

"But—" I floundered, panic and spiderwebs combining to squeeze the air from my lungs. "But how? I don't know where—"

"There is a Crone," he interrupted. "She has found a way across the barrier to where I came from—to where Grandmother Weaver still is. She can help you."

"Barrier? What barrier?"

"That which separated us from what we had created— until I opened the box and the darkness breached it. Now, there are holes. Gateways. The Crone can help you find one and cross it. Grandmother Weaver will be there. She can remake the box, but you must hurry. She is getting weaker, and her webs are already beginning to fray."

My mouth flapped open and shut as I grappled with the new information and considered and discarded a hundred questions. Dear sweet Mother of All, could he not have dropped at least some of this on me back at the monastery? Where my toes weren't slowly turning to cubes of ice, and the clock wasn't ticking inexorably toward our ride giving up on us and leaving?

I mean, he'd mentioned Grandmother Weaver before, yes, but he knew about the Crones? And was a gateway the same as the portal that Rebecca had told me about?

I snapped my teeth shut and closed my eyes for a second, taking in a deep breath through my nose as I tried to center myself and slow my chaotic, spiraling thoughts. Free of the scarf, however, my nostrils promptly froze shut, negating the attempt. I gave up and went with the first question I could put into words.

"How do you know all this?" I asked. "About the Crones and everything—and why haven't you said anything before?"

"I know much," he replied. "I've always known much because of what I am. Too much. But there was no point in sharing, because nothing could be done. *I* could do nothing."

Because of what he was. Not who, but what. My brain gave a little hiccup over that gem, but I pushed it aside for later mulling-over. I had neither the time nor the bandwidth for that level of philosophizing right now. And I really needed to get us down these stairs to meet Louis's aunt soon, and Methuselah was staring at the toy dragon he'd taken from his pocket, and I was losing him, and I still needed to know so much, and—

I placed a mittened hand on his arm, willing him to stay with me for a few moments more. "Where, Methuselah?" I asked, as gently as panic and despair would allow me to. "Where is the Crone?"

"There's a confluence somewhere," he said vaguely. "Phoenix is looking for it."

I was back to gaping at him, because Phoenix was *what?* But before I'd had time to digest his somewhat—hell, who was I kidding?—his *very* explosive announcement, his head snapped up.

"We must hurry," he muttered. "She's leaving."

"She who?" I croaked, still grappling with the Phoenix thing and nowhere near ready for another change of subject like this.

"Lucy," he said, stuffing the dragon back into his pocket. "Don't worry. I'll stop her."

"Luc—

Too late, it dawned on me who he meant. I made a grab for him as he turned away, but my hand closed on thin air, and the tall, ancient alien bolted down the stairs at a speed that would have sent me tumbling ass over teakettle if I attempted the same.

"Methuselah, no!" I shouted, but a blast of wind tore my words away from me and carried them into the old city, where the stone walls swallowed them. Not that Methuselah would have heard them anyway, because he had already disappeared down the remaining steps and vanished around the corner into the night along with his footsteps, and how in *hell* could he move so fast?

For an instant, panicked disbelief paralyzed me. I'd lost him. I'd lost the one being who knew the story of the stones and who'd said he could guide me to them, and—

The squeal of truck brakes and a long blast of an air horn shattered the night. My breath wheezed from my lungs, and my heart lurched down to my toes, ricocheted back up into my chest, and stopped working altogether for the space of several beats before it lurched back to life—along with my legs.

Well, I told myself—possibly with a touch of hysteria as I picked my way down the icy stairs at a fraction of Methuselah's speed—at least I'd found him again. Now, if only I could shake that feeling of being followed, all would be right in my world.

Well. As right as it could be. For a second or two. Until it wasn't again.

CHAPTER 22

WE'D ARRANGED TO MEET LOUIS'S *TANTE* LUCILLE ALONG THE road that paralleled the dock for the ferry to Lévis, one of the city's suburbs on the other side of the St. Lawrence. It was the same place where Louis had dropped me off on my first morning in Quebec City—after he'd rescued me from the rail-yard just outside Sainte-Foy, then driven me miles out of my way to Trois-Rivières on his run before returning me here. All while feeding me and giving me his coat to keep me warm.

It was like coming full circle, I thought, as I skidded to a stop on the icy sidewalk half a block away from a huge, cherry-red tractor-trailer stopped in the lane on the other side of the road.

Well, except for the part where Methuselah was currently planted in the road, inches in front of said tractor-trailer, while a tall, broadly proportioned figure waved its arms at him in unmistakable agitation. I hesitated, trying to size up the situation, then broke into a jog as a set of headlights approached from the opposite direction and began to slow. The Mages might not need to trace my movements anymore, but there was no point in advertising them, either. Whatever had happened before I'd arrived, I needed to de-escalate things before anyone else got involved and decided to call the cops, who might or might not have consortium ties.

I got to Methuselah just as the other vehicle—another semi—drew abreast of the unfolding scene. Taking the old man by the arm, I steered him over to the sidewalk and gave what I hoped looked like a reassuring wave instead of a *get lost* flap to the truck driver. To my relief, the semi rolled past, picked up speed, and rumbled away.

Relief ended with the clomp of booted feet coming up behind me.

"You're late," a gruff female voice informed me. "And he" —a pointed finger extended over my shoulder toward Methuselah—"damned near gave me a heart attack."

"*Rawr*," responded Methuselah, flying his dragon over to land on the truck's fender.

The pointing finger disappeared, and the woman—Louis's *tante* Lucille—grunted as she stepped forward to stand beside me. She slanted me a glance. "Dementia?"

I sighed. "Complicated," I said, watching the tall, fedora-ed old man fly the dragon across the headlight of the massive truck idling at the side of the road. He giggled at the enormous shadow cast across the road by the toy. The wise, all-knowing alien had once again been fully replaced by the child.

The gruff woman digested my response, and I took advantage of her distraction to size her up. She was the spitting image of her nephew, and only a fuller, rounder softness in her face would have set them apart had they stood side by side. The same mop of wild, steel-gray curls as his topped her head, and she had the same craggy lines around her eyes. She even had a similar build—that of, as Alice at the Mary Magdalene House for Women had liked to describe it, a brick shit-house.

She towered over me, not quite as tall as Methuselah, but not falling far short of him, either. No winter coat covered her broad shoulders, only a flannel shirt that hung loose over baggy jeans, and I shivered on her behalf as a blast of wind gusted in from the river. She, on the other hand, didn't even seem to notice it as she thrust her hand toward me for a handshake.

"Lucille," she said, unnecessarily confirming her identity.

I accepted automatically, replying just as unnecessarily, "Sister Monica."

A strong hand engulfed mine, then pulled back again as Louis's *tante* looked first startled and then sheepish.

"Sorry," she muttered, "but ..."

Her voice trailed off, and she stared down at my hand. Setting aside my surprise at the fact that, unlike her nephew, she spoke English with no discernible accent, I followed her gaze to the webs that had formed a mat across my burned palm. Right. I'd forgotten about those. But even as I sought for an explanation, Lucille let out a lengthy gust of air and raised her gaze to mine again.

"Let me guess," she said, with a tiny gesture toward my hand. "Complicated?"

"You have no idea."

She regarded me for a few seconds while Methuselah filled the otherwise silent night with a variety of dragon roars. All things considered, I was pretty sure she was questioning her involvement with us. Especially the part that meant she'd be in a confined space with me, Methuselah, and a toy dragon for several hours.

I studied her in turn, wondering about the wisdom of involving yet another unwitting bystander in the chaos intent on unfolding around me. Not knowing how I'd get to Ottawa without her.

"What Louis told me," she said abruptly. "About that night at the Citadelle. It was true? Ronald Drummond was there? And there were men throwing fireballs, and a monster made of ...?" She trailed off, pursed her lips, and shook her head, as if, nope, she just couldn't bring herself to say it.

I didn't blame her. I'd seen the goliath a half-dozen times now myself, and I still had trouble wrapping my head around a monster made of—

I shuddered at my memories of the monster. The memories of his screams echoing through the nights that I'd encountered him.

"Yes," I answered. "It's true. And, believe me, I'll understand if you don't want to get involved."

I'd be royally screwed, mind you, but I felt obligated to make the offer—a last-ditch out for her—and I *would* understand.

Lucille thought about it for another moment or so, then planted her hands on her broad hips, pursed her lips, and shook her head. "You know what?" she said. "I'll tell you what. That man is pure poison, and I would like nothing better than to help take him down. That *is* why you're going to Ottawa, right? To that global forum thingie?"

I blinked at her. She might have heard about the goliath from her nephew, but this? This, she had to have learned about from Sister Bernadette. The question was, this and what else? It hadn't occurred to me to ask the nun in the bustle of getting ready to leave, so I wasn't sure how much I could share with our ride. How much I *should* share.

On the other hand, I thought, as Methuselah roared again and Lucille's gaze flicked to him, there seemed no point in prevaricating about what she obviously already knew—or could see for herself.

"Yes," I confirmed. "That's why I'm going to Ottawa."

Lucille's voice and manner turned brisk. "Well, then. We'd better get moving. We have a long haul ahead of us. He"—she jabbed a thumb toward Methuselah—"can ride in the sleeper bed, and you can sit up front with me. I have questions."

And there ended the family resemblance between aunt and nephew, I thought, as she walked around the front of the truck to the driver's side. Louis and Lucille might look alike, but where he exuded a gruff gentleness and compassion, she was more like a force of nature—with an apparently impeccable grasp of the English language that would make dodging her questions … interesting.

My feet left the sidewalk as a blast of the air horn above my head made me jump. I bit back a surprised yelp and scowled up at the truck's windshield. Impeccable English, yes. Patience? Maybe not so much.

Curling my fingers around the stone embedded in my palm, I sent a last look over my shoulder at the old city that had sheltered me. At the lit-up façade of the Chateau Frontenac high on the hill above, beyond which, tucked into the midst of stone buildings and quiet, cobblestoned streets, sat the monastery—and the friends whose loss I would most definitely feel. The friends ... and Phoenix ...

And the Mages who watched them.

Lucille sounded another short blast of the horn, and I blinked back a blur of tears as I resolutely turned my attention back to the waiting truck, the ancient child-alien, and whatever came next.

CHAPTER 23

"*TABARNAK*," LUCILLE MUTTERED. SHE GLANCED AT THE driver's side mirror as she geared down for an approaching corner and added a vehement, "*Câlice*. Save me from asshole drivers."

I peered into the huge mirror on my own side but saw nothing. "Problem?"

"Only a jerk," she grumbled. "He's passed me a dozen times in the last half hour but keeps dropping back again like it's some kind of game. I'll tell you what, if you ask me, some people should never be allowed behind the wheel."

I frowned. I didn't expect Mages to interfere with us on our way to Ottawa—the consortium already had their plan in place for me, and Rebecca knew where I was heading, so neither of their groups had reason to follow me. But neither did I intend to court complacency, or to dismiss the possibility of rogue Mages acting on their own. Even without the other stones, Methuselah and I were valuable commodities.

Glancing over my shoulder into the sleeper cab behind the seats, I found an unperturbed Methuselah building mountains for his toy dragon out of Lucille's blankets and pillows and giving no indication that he sensed danger.

The stone, too, was quiet, and the spiderwebs beneath my skin lay dormant—which they wouldn't have done had the jerk of a driver been a Mage. My tightly coiled nerves released a fraction.

"You good?" Lucille asked, gearing down again as a handful of lights on the sides of buildings began sliding past us, heralding a return to civilization.

I nodded, then remembered she couldn't see me in the dark of the cab. "I'm fine," I said. "Just a bit wound up."

She grunted. "I wonder why."

I looked past my reflection in the side window and into the night. Once we'd settled into our respective places and Lucille had put the massive vehicle into motion, her questions had been fast, pointed, and unrelenting. They'd also been backed by what Louis had told her of that night at the Citadelle—and what Sister Bernadette had told her over the phone.

Dodging them had been … tricky.

By the time we'd crossed the bridge over the St. Lawrence River, she was sweet-talking me out of more information than I ever intended to give. Although sweet-talking might not have been the best way to describe her interrogation methods. Hell, Talia herself would have been impressed.

The shadowy profile behind the enormous steering wheel had tutted repeatedly when she learned that I planned to attempt a heist when we reached Ottawa. On my own. With just an old man who suffered from dementia as my sidekick.

"I'll tell you what," she'd muttered. "You going up against a man like Drummond by yourself just doesn't seem right. I have half a mind to—"

"I'll be fine," I'd interrupted hastily. "*We'll* be fine. We just need you to get us there, that's all."

Lucille had looked over her shoulder at Methuselah in the sleeper cab. "You and Matt," she'd said, calling him by the nickname the Ursulines had given him for public use and snorting her opinion of the idea that we'd be fine.

"You know what?" she'd continued, shaking her head as she turned her attention back to the road. "You're going to get yourselves arrested, is what. Or worse, killed by that monster thing Louis told me about. Or those fireballs the Mages can throw."

"I'm tougher than I look," I'd assured her, "and so is Meth —Matt."

At my near slip, she'd shot me a shrewd, narrow look— one that I couldn't see in the dark between us, but that I'd certainly been able to feel. Then, just as I'd braced for a new onslaught of questions, she'd abruptly changed topics.

Or, rather, tactics, but I'd been too relieved by the reprieve to realize it.

"My grandmother's sister was a nun," she'd said, changing lanes to pass one of the few vehicles that we'd encountered on the road. "An Ursuline. I'll tell you what, I thought about it myself once, but I decided I wasn't cut out for it. Always wondered what made a woman follow that path. Why did you?"

The question was innocuous enough—heaven knew I'd been asked many times before—and so it should have been easy to answer. But I mentioned her interrogation ability, right? In short order, Lucille had brushed aside my standard, pat, following-a-calling answer and drawn most of my before-the-stone life story from me with a finesse that bemused me.

What was most surprising, however, was the compassion that she hid behind her prickly exterior. Whenever my voice had caught on a rough edge of memory, she'd reached across the cab to place a hand on my knee—not in sympathy, but in a silent sharing of her own strength with me.

Both compassion and strength had been genuine, but the questions driving them had been calculated nonetheless, and slowly, she'd edged the conversation back toward Quebec City and how I'd come to be with the Ursulines.

I'd ended up telling her more than I would have liked but managed to keep it to only my involvement. Magick stone, one of a set, Drummond had the others and wanted to use them for nefarious purposes, that was why I had to steal them, blah blah blah. The fact that Louis had already told her about the Citadelle battle made it a little easier.

A little.

But trying to give her enough to satisfy her while keeping other details away was just more than my brain could handle. I could tell her about the stones, for instance, but the living darkness intent on devouring the entire universe and us with it? Probably not something I wanted to share with someone driving thousands of pounds down a dark winter highway at high speeds.

I'd finally feigned exhaustion as an excuse to tap out and lean against the passenger door with my coat as a pillow. Which had worked until I'd noticed her distraction with the vehicle that had been passing us and then dropping back again repeatedly, and had given myself away. Now, however …

I sighed and removed the coat from between me and the door, then reached around to deposit it on the bed in the sleeper cab. Methuselah immediately tugged it closer and turned it into a cave for his dragon, and I turned back to the windshield and the road ahead, casting a sideways glance at Lucille as I did.

Where, I wondered, had that strength she'd shared with me come from? I wasn't at all sure she would welcome a reciprocal sharing of histories, but perhaps I'd work up the nerve to ask later in the drive. At the very least, I was curious to know how she'd picked up such perfect English, and how she came to be driving a big rig at her age. And heaven knew the drive would be long enough, with the stops she had scheduled along the way.

I tried to remember the places she'd listed off as she'd spun the giant steering wheel first one way and then another to navigate onto the bridge out of Quebec City. Sherbrooke, I remembered, and then one that had sounded vaguely like Saint John Sirsomething—but I'd been distracted by getting Methuselah settled in the sleeper cab behind me, and I hadn't asked for clarification. I was pretty sure Cornwall was after that, which put us back in the province of Ontario with Ottawa only an hour and a bit further.

As for where we were at this moment?

I had no idea.

The truck was slowing again under her skilled hands and feet seamlessly working together to shift the gears down. Ahead of us, on the right, sat a brightly lit service station with giant bays for its gas pumps, a hand-lettered *CAFÉ* sign covering one window, and an enormous, paved parking area to one side. A vivid, lit-up red sign above the gas bar let everyone for miles know that it was open "24 h_u_es" (with two of the letters in *heures*, the French word for hours, burned out). The half-dozen other rigs in the lot were a testament to the stop's popularity among truckers along this less-traveled route.

Lucille wheeled into the parking area and pulled up in a spot next to another rig. I looked askance at her, because we'd made a pit stop at a similar, less populated place only an hour ago. I hadn't said anything to her at the time, but, given her nephew's creative use of an empty water bottle when I'd ridden with him, I'd been relieved to discover she believed in making actual stops. Still, another already?

Her lined face was set in annoyance. "You know what?" she growled, switching off the engine.

I'd already learned that she didn't expect an answer when she asked that particular question, and, sure enough, she continued without input from me.

"I'll tell you what," she said, unclasping her seatbelt as the truck rumbled into silence. "I've no patience for jackholes like that. Let him find someone else to play his games with. I'm going to get a coffee and a donut. You coming?"

"I—" I glanced back at Methuselah, weighed the odds of getting him in and out of the truck stop without drawing too much attention. Again, I wasn't overly concerned about Mages tracking us, but—

"Hello," Lucille said, her voice pitched low.

I blinked at her impatience and opened my mouth to tell her that Methuselah and I would wait in the truck, then paused. Her attention wasn't on me at all. It was on her side mirror again.

The hairs on the backs of my arms and neck lifted.

"Lucille?" I asked.

"They pulled in behind us," she said. "A black SUV—wait, the doors are opening. There's four of them—no, six of them—getting out. Two going around your side and—"

The rest of her words disappeared, swallowed by the rush of adrenaline through my veins as I swiveled my head to stare into my own mirror. Adrenaline … but still no webs.

What the fuck …?

I glimpsed faint movement in the mirror's reflection of the gap between Lucille's rig and the one she'd pulled up beside. The light from the powerful overhead lamps lining the parking area didn't reach into the space, however, and I couldn't make out anything useful. Then, in my peripheral vision, Lucille leaned down and pulled something from under her seat.

"No," I said, still watching my mirror as I put a hand out toward her. "It's safer if we stay inside the—"

The rest of my sentence disappeared in a garbled exclamation as my hand connected with—was that a *gun?*—and my head snapped around so fast that it felt like it might leave my shoulders.

"What the hell, Lucille!"

"It's only a stun gun," Lucille reassured me—although honestly, it wasn't that reassuring, because still freaking illegal. "And I'm not planning to get out of the truck, but I'll tell you what, I'm not letting them in, either."

She pried the weapon from my fingers and replaced it with a cell phone. "Call 911," she directed, "and tell them we're at—"

Something slammed against the door beside me, and I jumped. Sweet Mary Magdalene *and* Mother of All, who *were* these guys?

The stone remained dormant in my palm, and

Methuselah continued to swoop his dragon over the mountains he'd built. If neither of them was reacting, then at least we weren't dealing with Mages, but the good news ended there as another, harder blow struck the door beside me.

"We know you're in there, *sister*," a man's voice shouted. Young, by the sound of it, and—familiar?

I frowned, because that was impossible. I'd had neither the time nor the inclination to get to know anyone in Quebec City well enough to recognize their voice, and—

My entire center went still as I remembered, tried to reject the memory, and then stared it in the eye, because Holy Mother. It was *them*? Seriously?

Lucille was narrow-eyeing me. "You know these yahoos?"

"*Know* isn't the word I'd choose," I said, jerking my mind away from the porch of a cottage miles from anywhere and back to the present. Back to the impossibility and—regardless —the reality. "But yes, I've encountered them."

I looked over my shoulder at an unconcerned Methuselah. "Stay here," I told him. "With Lucille."

He gave no indication he'd heard, but Lucille did.

"Now hold on," she began.

My hand on the door handle, I cut her off. "Do *not* let him out, do you understand? No matter what happens. Promise me."

Louis's aunt bristled at being told what to do, looking rather like an offended cat as she narrowed her eyes at me. "I'll tell you what, young lady—"

Another blow slammed against the door, and the man's voice outside taunted, "Come out, come out, wherever you are, Sister! It's time to play again."

"*Promise* me," I repeated. "Please."

"Oh, for—"

We both flinched as a baseball bat smashed into the passenger window. The glass held, but the weapon's wielder was definitely escalating. Lucille's mouth pulled into a grim line, and she set the stun gun on the dashboard. She reached under the seat again, this time coming back up with a crowbar.

"Go," she said, holding it out to me. "And try to save at least some of my truck before the cops get here."

I hesitated. I didn't want the cops here, but I didn't have the time to explain why, and—and, oh hell. Now the café door had opened, and four burly men had marched out, and voices were bellowing, and—

Well. Even if Lucille didn't call 911, I'd lay dollars to donuts that someone inside already had. I grabbed the crowbar from Lucille, cast one last glance at Methuselah *rawring* softly to his dragon in the sleeper cab, and thrust open the door, issuing a final "*stay*," over my shoulder as I dropped to the ground.

My timing was as impeccable as it was lucky. The passenger door collided with the bat halfway through another swing, throwing the man brandishing it off balance and making him stagger toward the front of the truck. He recovered his footing there, but he lost the ill-fitting mask he'd been wearing in the process. A clown mask, I saw, as it lay on the ground in the beam from the headlights. How appropriate.

The group that had attacked me at the cottage in Kingston had worn masks, too.

Which made this what—an entire chuckle of clowns? Awesome.

CHAPTER 24

I DUCKED PAST THE TRUCK DOOR AND REACHED UP TO SLAM IT shut with my left hand, shifting the weight of the crowbar in my right, which for once held no stone, because there had been no reason to take it from my pocket. Yet. Then I did a quick scan of the surroundings.

Lucille had seen six people get out of the SUV that pulled in behind us. The chucklehead with the bat had been joined by four others—all hooded and with bats of their own—who held a quick, whispered consultation with him and then formed a protective semi-circle ten feet or so away from him against the approaching truckers.

Five out of six. That left one unaccounted for, but where? Were they on the other side of Lucille's rig? Or were they creeping around in the shadows behind me, waiting to strike?

I shifted so that the truck's giant front tire was at my back, then twisted my head to the right for a quick look down the dark alley between it and the rig beside it. Anyone—or anything—could be hiding in there. Or beneath one of trailers, for that matter. I needed to take this fight out into the open, and into the light.

Hefting the crowbar again—partly to find its perfect balance but mostly to look as threatening as I could—I moved to join the lead chucklehead in the high beams. There had been six of them at the cottage, too, I remembered: three men, one woman, and two who hadn't stuck around long enough to be identified. They'd come expecting an old woman who was frail and helpless, and instead they'd found a skilled martial artist with two black belts.

I'd used a shovel, that time. I'd found it leaning against the porch wall, and I'd broken the leg of one of the men with its handle. I'd taken out the knee of a second with a well-aimed kick, and I'd delivered a vicious uppercut—again with the shovel's handle—to their ringleader, knocking him out cold. A ringleader named—

Huh. My memory wasn't as bad as I thought it was sometimes.

"Hey, Aidan," I said, settling my feet against the hard, snow-packed pavement.

It was a guess on my part, but it was the only name the attackers had used at the cottage, screamed out by the woman with them when I'd laid him flat, so it was worth a shot.

"How did you—" He stopped himself, but it was too late. I'd guessed right. I smiled.

The burly truckers had stopped beyond the semi-circle of Aidan's bat-brandishing compatriots, hurling French invectives at the group interspersed with the words *police* and *allez*, which I recognized as *go* but in this instance sounded more like *get the fuck out of here.*

There was a smattering of *madames* thrown in, too, presumably aimed at me, but I ignored them, keeping my focus on my immediate foe and willing the truckers to remain at a distance. I didn't want to have to worry about them as well as Lucille and Methuselah.

"So, tell me, *Aidan*," I said, hefting the crowbar and making a deliberate show of twirling it gently, expertly—first in one hand and then the other. "What is so fucking important that you're willing to risk another beating from an old lady?"

Aidan gave a visible start at my language. Good. The more off balance he was, the better chance this old lady had of actually pulling off a second beating—or at least not taking one herself, the way she had last time.

"You know what I want," he said. "The same thing I wanted before."

I raised an eyebrow, making sure the truck's headlights illuminated my face. "And it took you almost three months to come looking for it? Or just that long to find me? Either way, wow. You're not exactly a go-getter, are you?"

That got him. He lunged at me, bat raised, but his swing was wild and I was ready. Metal crowbar connected with wood and sent the bat spinning from his grip. A concerned shout went up from the watching truckers. Applause followed. I pushed both to the edges of my consciousness as Aidan scrambled on hands and knees after his fallen weapon. He climbed back to his feet and whirled to face me, bat held across him like—well, like a bat.

That, however, was not what grabbed my attention.

The young man's hood had fallen back from his head in our little skirmish, and for the first time ever, in the light from the rig's headlights and the powerful lamps atop the poles that towered over the parking area, I got a look at his face. A good look. A look that told me that Aidan wasn't just any thug with a swaggering demeanor; he was quite possibly one of the most extraordinarily privileged thugs in existence, almost certainly one of the richest, and absolutely the most dangerous.

At least where I was concerned.

Because seriously?

The wet-behind-the-ears kid who kept coming after the stone and getting his balls handed to him on a plate (as Phoenix was fond of saying) was Aidan Drummond, son and only heir to Ronald Drummond, head Mage of the consortium?

"For fucksake," I said, because of course he was. And then I scowled at him. "Does your father know you're here?" I demanded.

"My father is none of your business," he snarled with a whine that assured me that no—no, Drummond did not know he was here. The idiot child was working on his own.

The idiot child swung the bat again. And missed again. "Just give me the stone, damn it!"

The weight of compassion joined the crowbar in my

grasp, and my hand drooped. "You don't know, do you?" I asked. "He hasn't told you anything, has he?"

Aidan's square jawline—made soft by the decadence of his life—went tight. "My father tells me everything," he said. "I know he wants the stone, and I know you have it and—"

"*That's* what this is about?" a new voice demanded. "Your daddy issues?"

Oh, hell. Lucille.

It would have taken all the willpower I possessed not to turn to her except for the fact that my attention was riveted on the rather interesting shade of purple that Aidan Drummond's face had suddenly turned.

"Fuck you!" he screeched. "Fuck you both! Give me the fucking stone or I swear, I'll—I'll—"

"Let it go, Aidan," one of the other clowns called out from the semi-circle, anxiety making his voice high pitched and squeaky. "I can hear sirens. We need to leave!"

"Stay where you are," Aidan shouted back, pointing in the clown's direction with his baseball bat even as his furious gaze held mine. "We're not leaving without that fucking stone, goddamn it!"

Sweet Mary Magdalene, he really didn't have a clue, did he? Or magick, I thought, checking in again with the inert stone sitting against my hip bone. He and his friends were just ordinary kids—well, maybe not so ordinary, but they were still kids and not Mages. Freaking hell, I didn't think they were even disciples, as Sister Margaret had once called the beginners.

And they wanted the stone? For what? To earn points from Daddy when they turned it over to—

My brain paused mid-thought as I stared at Aidan. Lucille came to stand by my shoulder, and I saw her open her mouth to speak, but I waved her silent. I stared at the oversized toddler brandishing the baseball bat at me.

"You want it for yourself," I murmured in shock. "You're

not planning to give it to your father. You want it for you. But even if I could give it to you, you wouldn't survive it. It would—"

"Shut up!" he screeched. "Shut up, shut up, shut up—you don't know that. You don't know what I'm capable of."

But I did, I thought. I knew all too well what he was capable of, and while the stone wasn't reacting to any magick in him, it wouldn't hesitate to swallow the darkness in him if he touched it. It would swallow him whole, and fucking hell, I didn't want it—or me—to do that, when that darkness wasn't even his in the first place. It belonged to his father, and to what his father had done to him, and—

I heaved an inward sigh, because I was going to have to cave to the inevitable and take out the little punk's knees, wasn't I? Shifting my grip and readying for a calculated attack, I made one last-ditch effort to dissuade him from disaster.

"You don't want to do this," I told him. "Seriously, Aidan. Do you not remember what happened last time?"

He let out a bitter guffaw. "Last time? Last time, you somehow got control over my father's monster, but look around"—he waved the baseball bat in a wide circle over his head—"because in case you haven't noticed, it's not here to help you this time. No one is here to help you. Now give me"—another wave of the bat, but in my direction this time—"the fucking stone."

"You know what?" Lucille grumbled beside me. "I'll tell you what. He's getting on my nerves, this one. Him and his friends. I say I take him down, and we hold him for the cops."

Before I could stop her, she waved the stun gun aloft, and what would have been merely disastrous turned catastrophic in the space of a heartbeat. One of the truckers dived to the ground with a shout—because yes, from a distance, an illegal stun gun looked just like a highly illegal handgun—and the others followed. The semi-circle of clowns broke and ran for cover, and shouts and bellows rang out across the parking lot, drowning out the still-distant but approaching sirens.

And worst of all? For a single, unforgivable instant, I let myself be distracted, and Aidan's baseball bat arced toward my head.

Decades of training saved my life. Instinctively, I threw my left arm up to take the blow, and the bat smashed into it instead of my skull, hard enough to split the skin and shatter the bones in my forearm. A wave of agony swept through me. Fury followed it, because again?

Sweet Mary Magdalene, I was getting tired of being a punching bag.

And I was pretty sure the stone was getting tired of it, too, because somewhere between the distraction of Lucille and the bat hitting my arm, I had dropped the crowbar and taken it from my pocket again. It bound itself to my palm, its webs uncoiling as Aidan danced back to give himself space for another swing at me. Some of them snaked beneath skin and through muscle to wrap around the bones in my shattered forearm, others pulled me inexorably toward the pavement, seeking the ground through which they could spread. All moving faster than they ever had before.

It took everything I had not to drop to my knees and slam my palm against the ice. Blinking back tears, I pushed back the pain radiating up my arm and fought for control of the webs, and then—

And then the missing sixth clown burst out of the shadows between the rigs with a high pitched, feminine scream—and a gun. A real one, aimed at the person nearest to her.

Lucille.

Time slowed to a fraction of its usual speed as instinct kicked in a second time. Forgetting all about the webs and the idiot they wanted to devour, I twisted to the right and threw myself between oncoming clown and aged aunt.

A single bullet tore through my breastbone and into my

body. It carried none of the force that Hollywood would have had me believe. It just … hit. There was no flying backward, no being lifted from my feet, no real fanfare of any kind.

It was quite anticlimactic, actually, a distant part of me observed.

There was simply a thud against my chest, followed by the sharp report of the gun's sound, and then I dropped to the ground like the proverbial sack of potatoes. The shouts and screams around me turned muffled. Then they went silent. Lucille leaned over me, her face frantic and her mouth moving as if forming words, but there was no sound.

Little by little, the world receded, dimmed, and then, like a tiny candle flame, it snuffed out. The last thing I saw was my outstretched hand, with the stone bound to it by its webs. My last certainty was that, even if it had been connected with the earth, it couldn't have saved me. Not this time.

Nothing could have.

Nothing, that was, except an alien, god-like being whose eyes held entire galaxies.

CHAPTER 25

AFTERWARD, LUCILLE WOULD TELL ME THAT METHUSELAH HAD swooped in, scooped up my limp form from the pavement, and let out a thunderous, rolling roar. That the sound had shattered every window in the café, the glass fronts on all the gas pumps, and the lights atop the lamp poles around us, and then a gust of wind had pushed away all the rigs but hers, tipping two of them onto their sides.

Then she would recount—with an unnerving level of glee in her voice—how Aidan and his asshat friends, as she called them, had all gone flying backward like the limp dicks they were—her words again, not mine. She'd tell me how they'd lain scattered around the parking lot, shrieking that all their bones were broken.

And *then*, she'd say, Methuselah had cradled me in one arm while he placed his other hand on my chest, and she'd tell me what, she'd never *seen* a light so bright, and it was coming from his eyes and his mouth and his nose like he'd been lit up like some kind of jack-o'-lantern, and she'd be damned if I hadn't just suddenly opened my eyes and started breathing again and taking charge and issuing orders and—

I shuddered now and drew deeper into the folds of the blanket that Lucille had given me, but it didn't help. No blanket could help the kind of cold that had settled into my core, because *holy fucking hell, Methuselah …*

The sound of his voice still reverberated through me. Through my very soul. I hadn't heard anything else, but I'd heard that. I hadn't been able to *not* hear it. It had reached out to envelop me in its demand, its sheer power, as it yanked me away from the edge of an abyss. From the promise of death.

"The truth is, we have no idea how powerful he is, or what he's capable of," whispered the memory of Sister Bernadette's voice.

I looked down at the thick, enormous flannel shirt Lucille had given me to replace my blood-soaked sweatshirt with the bullet hole in it, wondering what the Ursulines would say when they learned of this. If they ever would learn of it.

Lucille sent me another of her tight-lipped, sidelong looks as we rolled down the highway toward the pale dawn streaking the horizon. She hadn't been happy to leave the scene, but I hadn't cared, because there was no way we could have stayed to help. We hadn't dared.

Screaming forms had been strewn across the pavement amid shattered glass, tractor-trailers had been skewed in all directions with alarms blaring from three of them, and over the noise, the sirens had drawn closer. The noise hadn't been the worst part, though.

The worst part had been the silence. The open-mouthed, stunned silence of the truckers and the restaurant staff who had joined them to stare first at the destruction, and then at us.

To stare at me as I'd fought Methuselah's hold and he'd set me upright and I'd wobbled, finding my balance. To stare at Lucille, who'd stood to one side, stun gun dangling limply from one hand.

And to stare at Methuselah. Methuselah, who had sunk to his knees on the ice, whose eyes had turned to black pools that held no light at all and whose face had turned gaunt with grief and horror and—

I squeezed my eyes tight against the memory of his devastation—and the devastation that he'd caused—because dear sweet Mother of All, what *had* he done?

For long, interminable seconds, we'd all remained frozen, as if caught in limbo, and then one of the injured—the young woman—had whimpered, and all the truckers had been galvanized into action. Two had run toward the wrecked rigs from which I'd realized yet more screams were emanating—because six rigs in total and only four truckers in the restaurant, which meant—

I squeezed my eyes tighter, because Mary Magdalene, two others had still been in their trucks when Methuselah had—

I took a deep inhale and released it slowly to a count of four. Fuck. Fuck, fuck, *fuck*. But the calming technique did nothing, and my brain blithely picked up where it had left off. In my mind's eye, the replay of events continued.

The remaining truckers and the restaurant staff had headed toward the downed victims, and Lucille had made to follow. That was when I began barking the orders she had related back to me in her story, as if I might not remember. But I did, because how could I forget?

She'd dropped the stun gun to the ground and started toward the nearest form. It had been Aidan, lying in a pool of blood, and a sudden, cold horror had enveloped me. A terror. An absolute certainty that we needed to leave—*now*.

I'd yelled at her—not spoken, yelled—to leave the fallen man alone and get into the truck. She'd gaped at me in disbelief, and I'd bellowed the order a second time with the addition of a few *fucks* to get my point across.

"Leave him the fuck alone and get in the fucking truck fucking *now*," had been my exact words—so yes, pretty unforgettable.

Almost as unforgettable as walking away from the many people who needed help. But not nearly as unforgivable.

Lucille tried to argue, but an ear-blasting wail of sirens had swallowed her words as a fire truck turned into the truck stop. A cop car had slewed in sideways behind it, and we were out of time.

Swiftly, I'd picked up the stun gun and shoved it into her hands, put my face near hers, and gritted out, "Lucille. We cannot be here, do you understand? Whoever sent them"—I'd nodded at the injured clowns—"will come after us. We have to go."

It had been a little white lie, of course. I hadn't thought for a second that anyone had sent Aidan and his clowns after us. Drummond was too arrogant and far, far too confident in his plan. It would never have entered his mind that I might defy him. He would expect me to be weeping and wailing about poor Talia as I waited for further instructions—*his* instructions—not riding shotgun in a semi on my way to steal the rest of the stones from him.

But daddy issues aside, Aidan would make Drummond his one allotted phone call, and when he did, Drummond would know that I wasn't where I was supposed to be. He would realize that I was coming for him, and he might very well beat me to the proverbial punch, sending his Mages—or worse—to find and stop me. I had no intention of waiting to find out.

Lucille had still hesitated, of course. She wouldn't have been human if she hadn't. But then she'd looked at Methuselah, cowering against the rig's radiator grille, and then down at the illegal weapon she held, and then at my bloody sweatshirt. Finally, her gaze had lifted beyond my shoulder, her eyes had narrowed, and she'd given me a single nod.

"Fine," she'd said, her voice as hard as her jawline, "but I'll tell you what. I'm going to need a hell of a lot more information than what you've given me so far."

WE DIDN'T STOP AGAIN, AND REMARKABLY—MIRACULOUSLY— we weren't stopped, either. Not by any of the half-dozen cop cars that whizzed past us within minutes of our pulling back onto the highway. I held my breath at each set of flashing lights that approached, but none so much as slowed down, and then we were miles away and in the clear, and I could breathe normally again.

And I told Lucille everything.

Did I think involving her to that degree was the wisest course of action? Absolutely not, and if I'd seen any way around doing so, I would have taken it in a heartbeat. But she had seen too much for me to pretend that she could remain separate any longer—and I needed her too much.

Because I'd related most of my life story to her earlier, she already knew about my part in the unfolding events. Now I told her about Methuselah letting the darkness out of the box. I told her about the consortium of Mages that Drummond headed up and their quest to control all the stones and the alien who had brought them to our planet. I told her what Methuselah had said about Grandmother Weaver—the last of the Makers—being the only one who could restore the stones to their box form, and about her slowly being unmade by the darkness herself.

I talked, and Lucille listened, and the shadowed, snowy woods flashed by us on both sides of the road, interspersed with the occasional lone farm; and in the sleeper cab behind us, Methuselah said nothing. Did nothing. Moved not at all.

When I finished, Lucille's knuckles were white in their grip on the truck's giant steering wheel. She didn't speak for so long that I was beginning to think that what I'd told her had gone beyond her limits, and that she was debating whether to pull over now and dump us roadside, or to be kind and wait until we reached somewhere slightly more civilized before doing so.

This was why I hadn't wanted to tell her the full stor—

"I'm one of them, you know," she said abruptly, cutting off my thought.

Cutting off all my thoughts.

I stared at her. Blinked. Then said, "Pardon?"

Her jaw flexed in the light from the dashboard. "The Crones and midwitches you talked about. I'm one of them. Well. Related, anyway."

"You're—I don't understand. You're a Crone? A midwitch?"

"A witch," she corrected. "Solitary."

"I—I—" I didn't know what to say. How to respond. What to think. I'd heard the terms often enough to accept the existence of such women, but I hadn't thought beyond that existence. It had never entered my head that I might actually—

"Does Louis know?" I croaked.

Lucille cocked an eyebrow in my direction, then turned her attention back to the road. "Would that surprise you?"

Actually, no. In fact, it would go a long way toward explaining why he had been so unfazed by the Citadelle battle and the monster. And why he'd suggested *tante* Lucille as a candidate for the drive to Ottawa, now that I thought about it. Weird how the universe worked some days.

I stole a peek into the sleeper cab at Methuselah. Actually, knowing what I did now about the universe, perhaps it wasn't as weird as I'd once thought. I turned back to the road, smoothing the fingers of my empty hand over the flannel shirt that covered half my lap.

"What's the difference?" I asked. "Between them, I mean."

"Between midwitches and witches?" Lucille shrugged. "Not a lot, really. At least not at my age. Witches tend to be thought of as beginners. They become midwitches when they join covens and undergo formal training, but some of us aren't … group participants, I suppose you might say. We prefer to practice alone."

Lucille? Not a group participant? Very little could have shocked me less, but I kept the reaction to myself and asked, "And Crones?"

"Just as that Monterey woman told you. They're the most powerful, because they serve the Morrigan—or at least they did until the Fifth Crone came along and things got complicated. Before you ask, I don't know any more about it than that. Being solitary means just that. I have few connections to others."

The blunt statement made me wonder again about Lucille's life—and at the same time, made it abundantly clear that she was an intensely private person who would not welcome my questions. At least, not all of them.

One, however, I couldn't help asking.

"Your magick," I said. "What does it do? What can *you* do?"

To my surprise, Lucille chuckled with real amusement. "I'll tell you what," she said, "you didn't think this rig changed its color from red to blue all by itself now, did you?"

My gaze flashed to the hood of the truck outside the windshield, then to the side mirror, then back again, and I gave a little huff of surprise. She was right. The truck had been red when we'd met her in Quebec City—bright cherry red. I remembered it clearly. And now it was blue. And I'd been so caught up in … other stuff … that I hadn't even noticed.

"Neat trick," I murmured. No wonder the cop cars had sped past us without slowing down.

"It is, isn't it?" Lucille agreed rather smugly. "I do color magick, working with auras to help with healing or life changes, that sort of thing. Usually it's on human auras, but everything *has* an aura, so …" She trailed off with a shrug, then changed the subject. "How's the chest, by the way?"

I put a reflexive, protective hand up to where the flannel shirt covered the remains of the hole left by the bullet, my fingers probing the puckered indentation beneath the fabric. "It's better," I said. "Thank you."

"That's some healing capacity that stone of yours has."

"It's not—" I stopped. *It's not mine*, I'd been about to say, but the denial was unnecessary. The stone might not belong to me in a conventional sense, but for all intents and purposes, it was very much mine at the moment.

"Yes," I agreed, as Lucille flashed a sideways glance of inquiry that said she'd expected an answer. And that, at least, was true, because the speed with which the stone's webs healed me seemed to be getting faster and faster with each injury. Although I was fairly certain that Methuselah's intervention had made an impact on this last one.

I twisted around in my seat to peer into the shadowy depths of the sleeper cab. Methuselah was folded into the far corner behind Lucille, his arms locked around his knees as he sat and stared at nothing—or, at least, nothing that I could see. He looked much the same as he had when he'd been curled up in the monastery kitchen when Rebecca's Mages had taken up watch outside.

Only then, he'd been rocking back and forth. Now, he wasn't moving at all.

I considered crawling back into the sleeper cab with him, to hold his hand and talk to him the way I had in the kitchen —to talk him down from wherever he'd gone in his head—but I wasn't sure that I should. Or that I could. My fingertips still tingled from the energy that had zapped them when I'd touched his back at the truck stop.

I'd drawn back with a startled gasp, and the black gaze had fastened on mine.

"Don't," an ancient voice had rasped. "Don't touch. Dangerous. I am ... dangerous."

But I'd had no choice. I had to get him into the truck, and so, careful to avoid skin contact, I'd gritted my teeth and slid a hand beneath his elbow and helped him to his feet. I'd half-dragged him to the passenger door. I'd shoved him up and into the rig, then shoved him again into the sleeper cab before taking my own seat. Lucille had maneuvered the semi past the fire truck and police car and onto the highway as I snapped my seatbelt buckle into place, and we'd left the mayhem behind.

Methuselah's mayhem.

And now … now, unease rippled through me, and anxiety tightened my throat as I wondered just how dangerous he was.

And how broken.

CHAPTER 26

WE REACHED OTTAWA AT NOON. LUCILLE GUIDED THE enormous semi through Ottawa's crowded downtown core in silence, her skill and precision leaving me breathless. Or perhaps my breathlessness was due more to the number of parked cars, piles of snow that extended into the street in places, heavily bundled pedestrians who couldn't possibly see where they were going, and various other obstacles. I was sure we were going to wipe someone or something out, but Lucille managed to squeak the giant truck past everything without incident, and we ended up at the Government Conference Centre, where we needed to be. Or, at least, as close to it as we were going to get.

Because with a police barricade ahead of us to divert traffic, and two dump trucks parked nose-to-nose and sideways across the street beyond that, we'd reached the end of our road.

"Security," Lucille said tightly. "I can try to get us in another way, but they'll have done the same on all the other streets, too. And I'll tell you what, if they've gone to this trouble here, I can guarantee you they'll have even more security the closer you get to the building."

My breathing shallowed, and a shiver traveled over my skin despite the heat blasting from the fan beneath the dashboard. Rebecca had said that Drummond would have only Mages as security, but that had been before the incident with Aidan. Before he'd known that I was coming for the stones. Now, he expected me, he was prepared for me, and he knew that—unlike him—I wouldn't risk hurting civilians. And if he knew I was coming, there would have been nothing to stop him from sending his next message.

Talia.

Despair nibbled along the edges of the resolve that had carried me this far; defeat crowded behind it. I breathed through the urge to drop everything and find a phone, to call the monastery, to demand news. What was done was done, I told myself, pushing away the quiet, unrelenting terror. The heartache. I was here now, and I could change nothing in Quebec. The sisters and Phoenix would do what they had to, and I would do what *I* had to.

If I could get anywhere near the fucking stones.

If they were even here.

I looked back at Methuselah, hoping for a sign of some kind from him, but nope. He still wasn't moving. Sweet Mary Magdalene, but this heist was going sideways before it even got off the ground, wasn't it?

Determinedly, I returned my attention to the road before us. There had to be a way to do this. I just needed to figure it out.

I took quick stock of our location. To our left lay the sprawling center lawn of Parliament Hill, covered now in snow and flanked on three sides by the massive sandstone buildings that made up the seat of Canada's government; to our right, another massive, brown sandstone building that ran an entire city block. Ahead, a snarl of traffic waiting to turn the corner by the police barricade.

In a few moments, we would have no choice but to follow it.

"Are there other entrances to the center?" I asked.

"If memory serves, there are at least three, maybe four." Her head nodded in my peripheral vision. "But—"

"But those will be heavily guarded, too," I finished.

"They will."

"Fuck," I said, as my figure-it-out determination shriveled up around its edges.

"Fuck," Lucille agreed. Then she murmured thoughtfully,

"I'll tell you what, though. If we could create a diversion, it might draw enough of them away for you to slip inside. I mean, it's not like either of you looks particularly threatening. You'd be all but invisible with enough of a commotion going on."

"A magickal one?" I asked, brightening. "You could do that?"

She shook her head. "Not one big enough, no. And magick would warn them that you were coming. It needs to be something physical."

She had a point, but I had no way to create such a diversion. Sweet Mary Magdalene, one or two of the Ursulines' self-igniting Molotov cocktails would have come in handy right now. Although they'd probably have gotten me arrested before I got into the Government Conference Centre, too.

"I'll have to find another way," I said, shaking my head. "I'll call Phoenix and see if she can find out where Drummond might take the stones after the forum"—heaven help us if he returned to the States with them, but we'd cross that bridge when we came to it—"and we'll go from there."

"Or," said Lucille, reaching out to pat the dash in front of her with one hand as she swung the giant wheel around with the other to make the righthand turn at the police barricade, "Jean-Pierre and I can help."

LUCILLE'S IDEA WAS LUDICROUS, AND I TOLD HER SO IN NO uncertain terms.

"No," I said. "Absolutely not. There is no way in hell I am letting you ram your truck into those dump trucks. You'll kill yourself!"

"Rig," she said, placidly guiding the semi through the traffic of—

I glanced out the window at a street sign as we lumbered through an intersection. Elgin Street. We were on Elgin Street now, for what it was worth, and—

"What?" I asked.

"Jean-Pierre is a rig, not a truck," she said. She pointed out the window at an oncoming pickup. "*That* is a truck."

Really? She wanted to argue semantics right now, when she'd just proposed what amounted to a suicide run along the route we'd just come—down Wellington Street and past Parliament Hill, but blowing through the police barricade instead of turning at it? Because semantics were what was important?

I caught a glimpse of a sly smile playing across Lucille's lips and reined in my irritation. "You," I accused, "are trying to distract me, and the answer is still no. You and your *rig* are going to drop me and Methuselah off *here*"—I jabbed a finger toward the sidewalk—"and then leave, do you understand? This is not your fight, Lucille."

The smug, altogether too complacent woman behind the steering wheel maintained a steady speed, not even attempting to slow down, and shops and pedestrians continued to slip past on both sides.

"I'll tell you what," she said. "You need a distraction, I can create one, and you can't stop me."

"But I can fucking well refuse to participate."

"You can," she agreed, "but that would be a waste of an awfully good rig."

The urge to scream duked it out inside me with an equally strong urge to snort with laughter. I'd met few people in life who were more stubborn than I was. Talia had been—*was*—one of them. *Tante* Lucille, it was becoming apparent, was another.

The snort of laughter won, and Lucille grinned, looking decidedly Cheshire Cat-ish. I shook my head at her.

"Has anyone ever told you you're impossible?" I grumbled.

"They have," she said. "But I'll tell you what. At my age, I don't much care what other people think. Now, let's find somewhere we can sit and decide how best to do this, shall we? Lunch is on me."

CHAPTER 27

We ended up an hour west of Ottawa at a truck stop just off the highway, chosen after a short discussion for several reasons: ease of access (not counting the distance), amenities, and remoteness from Mages who might be able to sense my presence, or the stone's, or Methuselah's. Lucille was able to fill up the truck's—sorry, the *rig's*—fuel tank (for an astronomical amount of money), there were clean washroom facilities, and they had an onsite restaurant with better-than-decent food. My stomach audibly growled when the server set the all-day breakfast I'd ordered in front of me.

The middle-aged woman smiled and gave me a little wink as she set Lucille's plate down, too. "Enjoy," she said. "And wave if you need anything else."

We'd chosen a tiny corner booth as far from the door as we could get while still maintaining a view of the parking lot and Lucille's semi. I wasn't expecting trouble to follow us here, but, then again, my expectations of late hadn't exactly been on point.

Methuselah shared the wooden bench with me, wedged up against the window. I'd cautiously taken his hand to lead him into the restaurant with us, prepared for another jolt, but whatever energy had remained after saving my life—and destroying others, I thought with a shudder—had subsided. He was just an old man again.

Albeit an unspeaking one.

Across the table, Lucille tore off a corner of her toast and dipped it into a runny egg yolk on her plate. She watched me as I moved an egg and a slice of ham onto a small bread plate.

"You really think he'll eat?" she asked around her mouthful.

I slid the plate in front of Methuselah and lifted his hand to tuck a fork into it. He didn't resist. He also didn't react, and hand and fork both dropped back to his lap.

I met Lucille's gaze across the table. "He'll be okay," I said, picking up my own fork again. "He doesn't eat much as a rule."

That latter part was true. Methuselah's lack of appetite didn't worry me. I'd seen him go for days without eating and wasn't sure he actually needed to eat the way humans did.

The first part, though? About how he'd be okay? *That*, I worried about.

I wanted to see his lack of response to the world around him—to me—as a reaction to having lashed out and caused such destruction at the Quebec truck stop. As a sign of his attempt to remain in control. Because the alternative, the possibility that something in him—that his very mind—had been irretrievably lost …

I stuffed a piece of sausage in my mouth and chewed it fiercely, blinking back tears of overwhelm and fear and just plain exhaustion. Because if it was *that* alternative, how in hell was I ever going to get him into the conference center with me and keep him safe from the Mages?

WE PLANNED OUR ATTACK—LITERALLY—OVER COFFEE AFTER our table was cleared. Lucille pulled out her cell phone and opened the map app to display the area around the conference center. There was only one clear run that could be made toward the dump truck barricade, and that was down Wellington Street past Parliament Hill. We'd wait until the day's traffic had cleared, she decided, so that she could pick up enough speed to make the needed impact. She would drop me off on a run past the police barricade first, then circle back while Methuselah and I found the best place to wait.

"What if Drummond has already left the center?" I asked. "If they take the stones with them, this"—I pointed at the map on the phone—"will all be for nothing."

Lucille pursed her lips and frowned, then her brow cleared. "I'll tell you what," she said. "If they have the sidewalk closed to pedestrians on that side of the street"—it was her turn to jab a finger, this time at the Government Conference Centre building on the map—"you'll know everyone is still there. If it's open, they're gone for the day."

"We'll pick up a burner phone for you in the convenience store," she added, before I could raise the next issue. "That way, I can call you when I'm ready to make the run, and you can call me if I need to abort."

"And if we do need to abort?" I shivered at the thought of the consequences for Talia if Drummond learned that I'd tried to steal the stones. Would Rebecca's Mage still step in as promised? Would she be able to stop them from maiming the police detective? If she did, would the consortium then turn on the monastery and its occupants and trigger an all-out magickal war in the middle of Old Quebec? Hell, for all I knew, Drummond had already ordered them to do so after that Quebec truck stop fiasco with his son.

I swallowed hard and shook my head, because I couldn't go there. I needed to keep a clear head if any of this was going to stand a chance. I raised my gaze to Lucille's and said, "Time—"

"—is of the essence," she finished for me. She covered my hand with her own, the skin of her timeworn palm rough against the back of mine. "I know. But if my run at the barricade falls short ..."

"I'm fucked," I muttered.

"If you're right about all of this—if *he's* right," she replied, nodding at the unmoving Methuselah, still tucked in beside me, "then we're all screwed."

And so, because we really had no other options or ideas, our plan was made.

WE RETURNED TO THE RIG TO WAIT. IT HAD STARTED TO SNOW, and Lucille turned the vehicle on and left it idling to keep us warm. Methuselah went back to his place on the bed in the sleeper cab, this time lying on his back and staring up at the roof's interior, and Lucille reclined the driver's seat back and covered herself with a blanket pulled from the bed.

"I'll tell you what," she said as she made herself comfortable, "you should sleep, too. It's been a long day, and you're going to need your wits about you."

"I'll try," I said.

She grunted her doubts about that, closed her eyes, and was snoring in seconds. I checked on Methuselah, who hadn't moved, then turned back to watch the falling snow through the windshield.

It was coming down thick and fast, now. The footprints we'd left as we'd crossed the parking lot from the restaurant had already been erased, as if we'd never been here. As if they'd been swallowed up, the way Methuselah said the darkness was swallowing everything in its path.

The way the stone was swallowing me.

"You're feeding it too much."

I shivered—not with cold—and folded my arms across my belly. Lucille had told me that my seat reclined as well, but as wise as sleep would be, I couldn't bring myself to let down my guard. Couldn't risk Methuselah coming to life and slipping away. Couldn't stop scanning the vehicles that were coming and going. Couldn't stop thinking about the phone in the monastery that had rung, and rung, and rung with no answer when I'd used the burner phone I'd bought in the convenience store attached to the restaurant.

Calling them had been the first thing I'd done when I activated the phone.

Worrying about them had plagued me every nanosecond since.

Sweet Mary Magdalene, where could they be? I'd tried them twice from inside, twice more from the truck, and still nothing. I leaned my head back against the seat and stared at the snow piling up against the glass as a dozen scenarios played out in my imagination, none of them good. I thought about calling again, but there was no point. Whatever had been set in motion in Quebec was out of my hands, and to survive what came next, I needed to let go. Needed to—

"Belief is a powerful thing, Sister Monica," whispered the memory of Sister Bernadette's voice. *"It's … like intention when it comes to magick. The kind of intention that will carry you through, if you trust it."*

I drew a deep breath, held it a second, and then slowly exhaled. Yes, I thought. That. I needed to believe that the nuns and Phoenix and Talia were somehow okay, and that they were still able to believe in me. In me, in Methuselah, and in … that.

I opened my hand—the one tattooed with NO REGRETS—and gazed at the stone that had once more found its way into my spiderweb-healed palm. Symbiosis, I reminded myself. And damned if I wasn't beginning to believe in it, too. I closed my fingers over the stone and tucked my hand against my ribs, holding it in place with my other arm as I rested my shoulder against the truck door and stared out at the swirling snow.

Regrets or no, it was too late to change my path now.

My eyes closed.

When a hand settled on my shoulder, I nearly jumped out of my skin. Then I winced at the crick in my neck and the stiffness in the shoulder I'd been leaning on. Then I jolted upright. It was dark? How could it be dark? Oh, hell …

I'd fallen asleep.

Methuselah—

"Relax," Lucille said as I twisted my head around to peer into the back seat. "He's still there. Hasn't moved, I don't think. But it's time."

She tugged a snow-flecked toque from her head and dropped it onto the console between us, and I realized she'd been outside, clearing the snow from the rig. The wipers moved rhythmically across the windshield, keeping it clear. The parking lot had turned into a sea of white.

Lucille engaged the clutch and grasped the gear shift with one hand and the steering wheel with the other. She looked over at me. "Ready?"

I stared out at the winter night. No. No, I was not ready. I wasn't anywhere near ready. How could *anyone* be ready for this? But I nodded anyway. "Ready."

CHAPTER 28

There wasn't a lot to chat about, and so we made the hour-long drive back into the city in silence. Lucille, presumably, was preoccupied with how she was about to destroy her truck and risk her life, and I with going over and over the details of a plan that was too nebulous to have details.

Lucille dropped us off on Wellington Street, just shy of the police barricade that was redirecting traffic down Elgin. I slid out of the truck first, then helped Methuselah down—using the non-stone hand—to join me. He waited passively on the sidewalk, fedora in one hand and dragon in the other. I gazed through the falling snow, past the barricade toward the sideways dump trucks sitting under the bright streetlights, then I looked up at Lucille.

"You're sure about this?" I asked.

"That Jean-Pierre and I can cause a distraction?" She chuckled and slapped the giant steering wheel affectionately. "Oh, I'm sure, all right. You just be ready to move when you hear us hit."

"That wasn't what I meant."

She turned pensive as she stared out the windshield for a moment. Then, a tiny smile playing about her mouth and deepening the creases at the corner of her eyes, she glanced over at me.

"I'll tell you what," she replied. "I'm going to be eighty-four next month, and in my opinion, I've lived a full life. The world hasn't always made it an easy one, but it's been full. I've traveled, I've met and lost wonderful people, I've hit rock bottom and clawed my way back, and I have *lived*. I'd like to make sure that the world sticks around a while so that others have those same chances."

It took me a moment to clear my throat enough to respond.

"Fair," I said, because how on earth could I argue with that? Especially when I was about to walk into a viper's nest myself?

"Also," Lucille's smile widened to a grin, "in all that living I've done, I've never been arrested. It might be fun." With that, she adjusted the seat belt across her chest and hips, pulled it tight, and gave me a nod. "Now. Go get ready to save the world. I'll text you when I'm ready to roll."

A STILL-UNCOMMUNICATIVE BUT BLESSEDLY COOPERATIVE Methuselah and I waiting amid a collection of statues beside the Government Conference Centre, which stood across the street from the landmark Chateau Laurier hotel, The display was as close to our target as we'd been able to get, because the sidewalk in front of the conference center remained closed to pedestrians.

If Lucille was right, the barricades indicated that the forum participants were still inside, which complicated things enormously. Not for the consortium Mages, who would have no compunction about destroying innocent bystanders, but for me and the volatile Methuselah I could sense was holding on by a thread?

So complicated.

I huddled deeper into my coat, glancing upward at my companion's set, expressionless features. He stood beside the statue of a woman who held aloft what was meant to be the front page of a newspaper dated October 18, 1929. A dusting of snow topped the woman's hat, and the words *Women are persons* were emblazoned below the date on the bronze paper. I held back a derisive snort at the sheer irony of finding ourselves in the midst of a display honoring women who had led one of the many battles against the patriarchy, because here we were, almost a hundred years later, still fighting, and here *I* was, about to go to battle in the realest sense with the darkness that had helped to create it.

The long blast of a truck's air horn heralded Lucille's arrival. The sound of her semi's engine came next, its rumble growing louder as it roared down the street toward her target. Shouts of alarm went up as the police officers dived away from their barricade, and nearby pedestrians scrambled for safety—and then, like a rampaging elephant, the rig burst through.

It mowed over a police car as if the smaller vehicle were made of paper, shattering the wooden barriers, then bore down on the dump trucks. Lucille's aim was perfect, and her rig slammed between the trucks' nose-to-nose front ends. One of the trucks spun a hundred and eighty degrees under the impact, heading toward the sidewalk in front of the conference center; the other truck rolled completely onto its side and came to rest thirty feet down the street with Lucille's rig rammed up against it, her engine still roaring.

For an instant, shock held me immobile. Shock at the sheer violence, shock at how fast it happened, shock at how right Lucille had been when she'd said she could pick up enough speed to do serious damage. Then, as pedestrians and security guards alike erupted in screams and shouts, and a dozen armed figures converged on the rig, I grabbed Methuselah's arm. Beneath the cover of the milling crowd with their cameras and phones pointing in every direction, we ran out from the Famous Five statue display and into the shelter of the porticoed entry to the Government Conference Centre.

If Mages had been on guard at the entrance, we wouldn't have stood a chance. But to the agitated but very ordinary security guards gesturing at one another and shouting excitedly at their wrists, where microphones nestled under the cuffs of their suit jackets, we were just a frightened old woman and an even older man sheltering up against the building from an imminent threat. Then, as Lucille—dear, incredibly brave, Lucille—gave one last, unending blast of Jean-Pierre's air horn, the scant we attracted dissipated altogether, and we slipped behind the guards and through the doors.

Phase one was complete.

Panting from exertion and nerves, and with Methuselah's arm still firmly in my grasp, I skirted the handful of suit-clad people who had gathered in the lobby and headed further into the building. The conference center was housed in what had formerly been a train station, and before Methuselah and I had left Quebec, Phoenix had pulled up pictures on Sister Bernadette's computer so that I'd have some idea of the layout and where Drummond was most likely to be keeping the stones. I knew there would be a flight of stairs from the small lobby down to a larger, more open space—once the general waiting room of the train station.

Phoenix had also researched the forum itself, so I also knew that almost five hundred participants were expected. What I hadn't expected was to find what looked like most of those five hundred milling about in that single space in a panic as they shouted out rumors of an attack outside the center. Phase two lurched to an uncertain halt as we stopped on the broad landing halfway down the marble stairs.

I stared down at the sea of people between me and the conference rooms that Phoenix's research had identified further into the building. Two of those rooms stood on either side of the waiting room, both clad in bronze panels, with others beyond the wall of glass doors at the far end. Which of them was most likely to house the stones and the Mages who guarded them, and quite possibly Drummond himself, I had no idea.

My gaze darted left, right, up, and back down again, but

there was no clear path through the tightly wedged-together bodies. There was also no way for me to separate Mage from magic-less human—foe from lesser foe, given that anyone attending a consortium-hosted event wasn't likely to be a friend, but I still didn't want to cause unnecessary damage.

We would go around the perimeter, I decided. It would take a little longer, but it would draw less attention to us than pushing our way through. My lips tightened, as did my hand on Methuselah's arm as he stirred beside me. I didn't dare let us get separated.

I turned to tell him the plan, but before I could speak, a portly man with three chins, a ruddy face, and sweat beading on his brow shoved past me, almost knocking me down the marble stairs. I let go of Methuselah and flailed my arms to regain my balance, not because I was afraid of injury—the stone would take care of that—but because Drummond and his minions weren't stupid. They would have figured out by now that I'd arrived, and they'd be actively searching for me. And while an old lady in a crowd might go unnoticed, an old lady tumbling down a flight of marble stairs would not.

The sound of approaching sirens came through the doors and across the small lobby, reminding me that time was of the essence. I needed to get to the stones before they were moved —if they hadn't been already.

But even as I took Methuselah's sleeve again, his head snapped up, his gaze locked onto the door of the bronze-clad room on the righthand side of the general waiting room, and he tugged away from my fingertips.

I stared after him as he loped down the stairs. Shit. So much for not getting separated.

I jogged after him, unbuttoning and shedding my coat as I went. Whatever resistance we might meet, I wanted unrestricted movement.

Methuselah had reached the bottom of the stairs and begun pushing his way through the crowd. There was a brief stir of annoyance, and then people began to give way before the tall, ancient, fedora-ed alien, falling silent as he passed and turning to follow his progress. So much for not drawing attention, too.

I dropped my coat and scarf into the base of a nearby planter and leapt to follow my companion as the crowd drifted closed behind him again. Catching up, I slipped my hand into the crook of his arm and tucked myself in as close as I could to his back without stepping on his heels.

"Are they here?" I wanted to ask. *"Can you feel them?"*

But even if he could have heard me over the babble of voices, he wasn't likely to answer, and, really, did I need to ask at all? He'd told me that he could feel the stones, that they called to him, and the fact that he was moving with such purpose in such a decisive direction—

As abruptly as he'd started walking, Methuselah stopped again, and I face-planted into his trench coat-clad back. Before I could recover my balance, he stretched both his hands out to his sides, paused, and then clapped them together. A sound like thunder rolled through the vaulted room and screaming people dived to the floor all around us—

Except for three who stood between Methuselah and a closed door that glowed with an eerie, sickly green light.

We had, it seemed, found what we were looking for.

Along with the Mages who were guarding it.

CHAPTER 29

Power crackled through the air, snapping against my skin like tiny sparks of electricity. It took me a second to realize that it came not from the Mages, but from the alien standing with his back to me—and that it was intensifying.

A dozen thoughts took shape in my skull at the same time.

Let him, one of them said. *Let him destroy them.*

Let him, another agreed. *Let him take the stones.*

Let him, said a third. *It's his responsibility.*

What about the people? Remember the truck stop, said a fourth.

Fuck, said a fifth. *You have to do something.*

"Bomb!" I bellowed, because it was the first thing that popped into my head—aside from the voices—and I'd used a similar tactic before, on the train to Quebec City, and—

I realized my mistake almost instantly.

Because this was nothing like that had been.

It was the train all over again, yes—but on steroids. When I'd shouted out the threat there, it had galvanized a couple of dozen people out of their seats and into a narrow aisle with only one way out—and with a rail employee on hand to supervise their exit, no less. It had been calm. Orderly. Swift.

This ... this was pandemonium. The roughly three hundred people who'd thrown themselves to the tile floor only a moment before surged to their feet *en masse* and began shoving wildly in every direction. A woman a few feet away from me fell to her knees, and only the quick intervention of her companion kept her from being trampled by the panicked feet of dozens. I watched in helpless horror as others staggered and pushed and screamed.

Sweet Mary Magdalene, what had I done?

From the corner of my eye, I saw Methuselah's hands part

again, and I threw myself at him, hanging on for dear life to one outstretched arm. Hanging on for *all* life.

"Stop!" I yelled at him. "Methuselah, stop! This isn't how——"

A crimson fireball rolled past my ear, cast by one of the Mages guarding the room, and exploded against the opposite wall. Methuselah's hands slammed together again, carrying me along for the ride as if I wasn't dangling from one of them, feet off the floor. While nothing visible emanated from the alien's hands, a second rumble went through the building, this one more like an earthquake than thunder.

And, like an earthquake, it shook the very foundation.

The ornate ceiling above the waiting room cracked, sending chunks of plaster plummeting into the crowd below, and I looked over my shoulder to see the crystal chandeliers at the base of the stairs swinging wildly. One of them crashed to the floor, shattering with a sharp, discordant disharmony above the crowd's screams as the same floor rolled beneath stampeding feet. The green-glowing door blasted into the room behind it as if I'd been right about a bomb, taking the three Mage guards with it. Instantly, a strident klaxon shrieked at a pitch and volume that made everyone in the vicinity clap hands over ears, including me.

Then the real fun began.

The three Mages who had been hurled into the room with the door staggered to their feet, one of them bleeding from a cut on his forehead, another from his nose. All looked stunned. And all were trying to keep themselves between Methuselah and the only object in the room: a glass display case on a pedestal at the back.

Unfortunately for them, the four other Mages bursting into the room through a side door didn't stop to consider that the intruders might be their own. The new arrivals launched red fireballs, and the three Mage guards went down—literally —in flames.

Flames into which Methuselah thrust me without hesitation as he pushed me toward the glass case and the small black strongbox it contained—and ahead of a half dozen more Mages who were coming in hot behind us. Methuselah ignored them all.

We reached the pedestal, and I ducked away from an exchange of fireballs crackling past my ear. Shock registered as Methuselah raised a fist to smash the glass case, because wait—some of those fireballs were blue, not red. Where had they come from? And the klaxon alarm had abruptly cut off, but a screeching outside in the lobby had taken its place, drowning out the panicked screams and cries, and sweet Mary Magdalene—

I'd heard that screech before.

Serpent, I remembered. But then glass shards rained across the floor, and I forgot again.

"Stop," I choked out as Methuselah reached to take the box. "You can't."

He hesitated, and his hand hovered above the metal cube.

"Get them, Sister Monica," a familiar woman's voice called. "Get the stones and get out! We can't hold them back for—"

Rebecca Monterey's words were cut off by another screech. Brilliant red exploded to my right, blue to my left, and flames spread to engulf the wall, licking toward the ceiling.

"Do *not* harm them!" another voice commanded, male this time. "You're to take them both alive, do you hear me?"

Drummond, I thought. Goddamn, fucking Drummond.

Sudden fury consumed me and, forgetting Methuselah for

a second, I whirled to face the man who was behind all of this and so much more. Talia's kidnapping; the deaths of the women of the Mary Magdalene House and those of the nuns who had called me sister in Toronto; the havoc that had been wreaked in Kingston and Quebec City and now here.

The overt hatred that had crawled out of the world's proverbial woodwork, emboldened by his presence and encouragement. The pain and misery that had been inflicted in the name of that hatred.

All of that and more was because of him. Because of the darkness he carried within him, the darkness that he had willingly become. The darkness that the stone wanted. The stone that was no longer in my pocket, but in my hand.

Its webs came alive in me, and it grew warm in my palm. I crouched and stretched my hand toward the floor, oblivious to the magick crackling back and forth between the two Mage factions as I focused on my foe, but just as my knuckles brushed the tile, something stopped me. A hand ... first on my shoulder, then sliding beneath my arm, then lifting me to my feet again.

"Stop," Methuselah said, echoing my words of a moment before in the first he'd spoken since the Quebec truck stop. "You can't."

I almost didn't heed him. The stone almost didn't let me. But then I met the alien's gaze, and the hunger in me dimmed in the face of something greater. Greater than me, greater than the stone. Greater than both of us together.

The galaxies were again in Methuselah's eyes, but not as they had been before. These ones roiled and seethed, churning far away in impossible depths and then rushing toward me as if they would swallow me whole. And, interspersed between the galaxies, holding them both together and apart, I saw the ache of yearning, and loss, and regret.

My breath turned sharp as I inhaled. So much regret.

My gaze shifted to Drummond's back as he retreated out

the side door, some of his Mages following to protect his exit while others remained to fight his battle for him. *Coward,* I thought. *Goddamn, fucking* coward.

But I had no time to dwell on his disappearance. From the corner of my eye, I saw Rebecca's Mages fall back through the other door to the lobby, alight with cerulean and crimson flames. The serpent screeched again. We needed to end this, I thought, before they brought the entire building down around our ears and their war spread into the city beyond.

I turned and reached past Methuselah with my free hand to snatch up the strongbox from its pedestal. I leaned close to speak into his ear over the din of battle.

"Can you help me get out of here?" I asked. "There are too many, and I don't think I should—" I waved the box aloft and flinched as the stones rattled inside it. I was half-elated that I hadn't been enveloped in a giant, exploding cocoon the instant I'd touched it. Mostly relieved. And I had no intention of pushing my luck.

The galaxies threatened to swallow me again, and Methuselah made a visible effort to straighten shoulders bowed under the weight he had carried for far too long.

"I'm fading," he said quietly. "Faster than I thought I would. But I'll try. Stay close."

I tucked myself in behind him as he strode back the way we'd come in.

WE MADE IT AS FAR AS THE LONG WOODEN BENCH—A REMNANT of a bygone era—in the center of the waiting room.

Rebecca's Mages had raced to shelter in the bronze room on the left-hand side of the vaulted space. Drummond's Mages were more plentiful. Some remained in the room that was mostly on fire, while others blocked our path through the wall of glass doors leading to the rest of the building. The many-human-headed serpent—which was just as horrifying here as it had been in the square behind Notre Dame Cathedral in Quebec when I'd first seen it—shrieked from the top of the stairs that led up to the street and our only other exit.

The only bright side was that the lobby was empty except for the Mage combatants. Despite the monster they'd faced—or perhaps because of it—the civilians had managed to get away in our absence. Well, most of them, anyway. My gaze feathered over a few prone, unmoving figures, not pausing, not counting, as I sheltered on Rebecca's side of the wooden bench, tucked the strongbox close against my ribs and scanned the space for a way out.

There was none.

And the pause in the lobbing of fireballs from the Drummond side toward Rebecca's did not bode well. Although, I decided as crimson slammed into the far end of the bench and spread toward my head, I definitely preferred a pause to a direct attack.

A second red fireball landed on the floor to our right, smashing a crater into it and spraying us with marble shards. Methuselah put himself between me and the flames, and I hugged the box tighter, curling my shoulders around it.

The serpent screeched, and one of its human heads, which had long snake-like fangs—had I noticed those before?—waved toward the stairs as if seeking a path down to us.

"We can't stay here," I shouted over it. "They're trying to drive us toward that." I nodded at the serpent while keeping one eye on the consortium Mages blocking us from going further into the building—and accessing the other exits Phoenix had pointed out when we'd studied the photos on the internet together. Trying to get past them might be our best bet, especially since they'd been told to take us alive. It was better than trying to get past the throngs of security and gawkers beyond the serpent, assuming we evaded it in the first place.

I touched Methuselah's shoulder and pointed at the Mages and the glass doors. "That way is our best chance," I said. "On three. One, two, thr—"

My words ended in a shout of pain as a new crimson fireball rolled toward us and a cerulean one intercepted it. Purple flames exploded from the collision, washing over me and tearing the strongbox from my hands. Again Methuselah stepped in to protect me, but it was too late. The box spun away across the tiles, coming to rest in the middle of the waiting room floor, halfway between the warring Mage factions. Its lid was gone, and its sides had melted into a twisted ruin of metal.

Five pieces of obsidian sat unscathed at its center.

Fuck, I thought. I blinked away the tears of pain as the stone's webs spread through me, seeking the cause. Fuck, fuck, *fuck.*

Above me, Methuselah said, "It's time."

I pulled my head back from trying to peer around the pillar. Rebecca's Mages were doing their best to draw the fire of the others, but the consortium's Mages were staying focused on me and Methuselah, except for the one crawling toward the stones on the floor, and—

"Time?" I asked. "Time for what?"

"Remember your promise," he said. Then, turning his head, he looked down at me from beneath the rim of his fedora. The galaxies in his eyes were gone, replaced by what looked like the supernovas that I'd seen in television documentaries, and I almost choked on my inhale.

"Methuselah?" I squeaked, but he spoke again before I could say anything more. Before I could come up with anything *to* say.

"Tell Grandmother that I'm sorry," he said. "And now, *run.*"

With that, and as the serpent shrieked again, he stepped back from the pillar, standing tall with his shoulders squared and his arms relaxed at his sides. Explosions of color radiated outward, brilliant and beautiful, first from his eyes and then from him—one after another after another. The consortium Mages who were in the open and trying to crawl to the stones stood and turned to run. They didn't make it.

The colors streaming from the alien slammed into the walls, the floor, the vaulted ceiling—the exit. Waves of energy rolled outward, driving those Mages unfortunate enough to be caught by it headfirst through the wall of plate-glass doors. The many-headed serpent wailed and slithered toward the upper street exit as the very building itself rained down on us.

The Mages lucky enough to find shelter in the bronze-clad rooms or the nooks to either side curled into tight balls of flesh and terror as they waited for it to end.

It did, of course. There was only so much of the alien that could be taken apart. Only so much undoing that could be done. The waves of colors streaming from him became faint ribbons and threads of silver, purple, blue, green—every color and hue imaginable, every color and hue that existed. They unraveled from him until there were no more to unravel, and then slowly, as if he somehow still occupied them and had just become tired and wanted to sit, his empty clothes sank to the floor.

I watched through a blur of loss as the last threads drifted away and joined the ribbons of light that danced and wove through the ruined lobby. The ribbons brightened, faded, then vanished. He was gone.

Utter silence reigned for a long moment, punctuated by a falling chunk of plaster here, a screaming serpent-head there. It didn't last.

"The stones!" someone cried, and the battle of the Mages was on again.

CHAPTER 30

Lifting my gaze from the empty clothes on the floor, I turned my head one way and then the other, taking in the mayhem. The hatred. The blind drive to win. All around me, opposing Mages continued to lob fireballs and arcs of brilliant magick at one another, fighting for possession of the stones, oblivious to the loss of the being who had brought them.

The beautiful, broken being who had been forged of the stuff of creation itself, who had chosen to unmake himself to save me. To save what was left of the world despite how far gone we already were. And now, it was up to me.

Me, with my back to a pillar and all but surrounded by my enemies, and the box of stones lying open in the middle of the rubble-strewn floor—which felt like half a world away. The consortium fanned out on one side of me and Rebecca's collective on the other, and the many-human-headed serpent hissed and screeched outside the shattered glass doors, keeping the police at bay. New sirens signaled the arrival of reinforcements.

"Promise me," the memory of Methuselah whispered.

But I couldn't. Not like this. Not with no way out.

A soul-sucking, desperate desire for power permeated the air, sickly sweet in my nostrils, bitter on my tongue, and the darkness in me rose eagerly to taste it. I pushed it down again. *Enough,* I thought.

And then, "Enough!" I roared.

Fireballs dropped to the floor, halfway to their intended targets as my bellow ricocheted through the vaulted lobby, shattering the Mages' concentration. Heads snapped around and ten pairs of startled eyes fastened on me. Energy pulsed through the air and between fingers on hands still raised for battle. Six Mages on Rebecca's side, four on the consortium's.

"Enough," I repeated, quietly, wearily. "It's over. Don't you understand? Methuselah is gone. No one can control the stones anymore. Not any of you. It's done."

A Mage who I recognized as one of Drummond's personal guards from the room where we'd found the stones lowered his hands and took a step forward.

"Then it won't matter if we take them." Young and eager, he jutted his chin toward the pile, and his avaricious gaze flicked from me to it and back again. "Since you think they're so useless, I mean."

"I think not," answered Rebecca's voice before I could.

It was probably better that she'd replied, since the response forming on my own tongue had been more along the lines of *over my fucking dead body*. I turned my head, seeking her amid the shadows of the disaster. She stepped away from the far wall, into the light of the flames burning along the length of a pillar—our only light, now that she and her cohorts had destroyed the electricity, along with most of the building.

"The stones belong to us, now," she reminded me, her own head tilted in challenge. Her hair was awry and the front of her dress streaked with dust, but her lipstick—somehow and impossibly—was still intact as she pursed her lips. "We have an agreement."

Immediate dissent filled the air, with both sides shouting that they couldn't trust the other and demanding that they be the ones to be the stones' caretakers. The lack of their ability —on both sides—to see the irony of their arguments was stunning. Not surprising, perhaps, but still stunning.

"Tell them, Monica," Rebecca demanded, raising her voice over the others. "Tell them we have an agreement."

I closed my eyes. I breathed. I thought of how I would weep for Talia later—and for the rest of my existence. And then I stepped fully into the decision I had made at a hotel restaurant lunch table, perhaps even before that. Stepped into it, owned it, and denied my very heart in doing so.

"*You* had an agreement," I corrected Rebecca, opening my eyes again. "*I* have a promise to keep that supersedes it. And my name is *Sister* Monica."

"*Promise me*," Methuselah's lost voice whispered in my ear. "*Promise you will find Grandmother Weaver and save her.*"

"*I promise.*"

Hands came up again on all sides, and a renewed crackle of energy went through the gathering. Rebecca drew herself up to her full height—an impressive one with the added four inches of her high heels, which she'd somehow retained along with her lipstick.

"A promise to whom?"

I nodded at the empty clothes in front of me. "To someone far greater than you can ever hope to be," I said.

Then, because I wanted to believe that there was some good still in the woman I'd formed an alliance with—and I really, really didn't want to have to fight my way out of here and spend the rest of my existence looking over my shoulder or jumping at shadows—I told her about the stones' origins and about the living darkness and the dying Weaver.

When I finished Methuselah's story, the entire lobby was silent. For the first time, I saw doubt written across the faces of not just one Mage, the one I'd been talking to, but across several. On both sides. Doubt … and hesitation. There was another shuffling of feet against gritty tile as stances shifted.

Her expression poker-champion still, Rebecca stared at me. "You're sure," she said finally. "You're sure what he told you was true."

A small, sad guffaw escaped me, and I found myself blinking back tears. I sniffled and waved my hand at the ruined building around us, then wider in an effort to encompass the world beyond.

"Look around us, Rebecca," I said. "*Look* at the shape the

world is in. We're crumbling. Everything around us is falling apart, because something is seriously, seriously wrong, and if we don't fix it, if we don't fix whatever it is, it will destroy us. It will destroy everything. You *must* see that."

The lines at the corners of her eyes tightened. Just a fraction, but it was enough to tell me that she was listening. That she was hearing me. That she might be swayed. I pressed on, pointing to the strongbox amid the rubble.

"Let me try to change it," I said. "Let me try to change the path we're on and—"

I didn't have a chance to finish—or to find out whether I might have convinced her.

A seething ball of crimson smashed into me, launched by the consortium Mage nearest me—Drummond's puppy. It lifted me off my feet and slammed me backward into the wall twenty feet away, hard enough to knock the wind from my lungs. Hard enough that my head connected with marble, and sparks of light went off behind my eyelids, and the stone sent its webs spinning through me to cushion my brain from the resulting bounce against my skull.

By the time I hauled myself upright again through the fog and the almost unbearable ringing in my ears, Mages from both warring factions had dived for the strongbox. Drummond's puppy got there first, snatching the box from the floor. He fumbled it immediately, however, and the box dropped again to the tiles, its obsidian treasure scattering.

If there had been chaos before, there was sheer bedlam now.

Mages hit the floor on both sides, scrabbling across the marble in every direction in pursuit of the stones, trying to protect their treasures while not touching them. Suit jackets and ties came off to provide makeshift barriers between skin and devastation, and spheres of fire were lobbed left and right without aim.

One misguided blast streaked up the stairs and hit the

front entrance, shattering the glass there and enveloping the many-headed serpent. An unholy screech erupted from it, and its writhing tail swept a cascade of fallen plaster chunks over the waiting room, narrowly missing my head.

Even Rebecca, in her fitted dress and high heels, had lost both dignity and sense as she flung herself toward Drummond's puppy. So much for appealing to her better judgment.

Fuck.

Fuck, fuck, fuck … and now what?

Fresh screams came from the street above and outside, and a dull part of me noted that the serpent had slithered away and out the door. Dull, because there was nothing I could do about it. I needed to choose my battles, and that—despite the lives that might be lost—could not be one of them.

Gritting my teeth, I wobbled my way back to Methuselah's empty clothing and sank down beside it, fighting back the webs that had wound themselves around my cerebrum. They recoiled, but far, far too slowly for my liking—because dear sweet Mary Magdalene, they were in my *head*—and I put my hands to my ringing ears, then yelped and dropped them again as the stone I held tucked in my right palm scorched my earlobe, its message unmistakable.

I clenched my fist around it, refusing to comply. Terrified to do so. There were too many civilians outside who had nothing to do with this magickal war, who didn't even know about it—although I supposed they might have surmised at least something by now, what with the many-headed serpent that had just appeared in their midst.

Even as I fought for control, however, the Mages were becoming increasingly unhinged. Increasingly desperate. The opposing factions jealously guarded two stones each, and the last bit of obsidian sat halfway between them. I had to do something, before the very magick they tossed at one another brought down the remainder of the building around us.

Because the stone in my hand was done taking *no* for an answer.

CHAPTER 31

THE STONE'S HEAT SPREAD UP FROM MY PALM TO MY WRIST, then traveled up my arm. Its advance was relentless. Focused. Determined. I stopped trying to stop it and concentrated instead on containing it. Controlling it.

As if.

Under cover of a volley of fireballs launched by his colleagues, a consortium Mage scrambled on all fours toward the last remaining stone. A blast of cerulean hit his head and set his hair alight, and he rolled across the floor, squealing in agony. Of its own accord, my hand slammed to the floor beside me.

Webs shot outward.

Stop, I thought at them. At the stone. At myself. But no one listened. My other hand brushed against Methuselah's coat beside me, and my fingers curled into its folds, holding tight to it, as if it might anchor me. Us.

"Promise me," Methuselah whispered.

The webs had reached the Mages and began binding them to the floor. Shouts of panic battered my ears, and a wave of helplessness began to swamp me. Helplessness, despair, anguish. Inside my very core, a deep, bottomless, vast darkness yawned, beckoning me toward it, infinite in its promise of—

"Promise," said Methuselah again.

Irritation sparked. Fucking holy everything that ever was or would be or *could* be—what did he expect me to do? It wasn't like I could just reach out and take the stones back, for fucksake. The webs had already—

My brain paused, then replayed my last few thoughts. A tiny glimmer of hope popped up beside the irritation.

Sweet Mary Magdalene.

That was it. The webs.

Curling my hand tighter into Methuselah's empty coat, I clenched my jaw, gritting my teeth so hard that stabs of pain jolted through them. I closed my eyes. The darkness unfolded wider. Bigger. Deeper. In my mind, I took a step back from it. Then another step.

From out in the street came the sound of an explosion, then the serpent screaming in pain, then another explosion. Curiosity tugged at me. I turned away from it.

A Mage on the consortium's side of the battle shrieked in terror. I shut out the sound. Rebecca shouted my name. I ignored her, too. The stone's heat continued to spread through me. I let it.

For the first time, I didn't fear it. I didn't think about what it might do to me, because it wasn't about me. It was about more. It was about Phoenix and Talia and the sisters, it was about the civilians outside the shattered doors and the city beyond them and all the cities and towns and people beyond that. It was about Earth itself, and the galaxies reflected in Methuselah's eyes, and the Maker—the Weaver—who had woven them all.

Because Methuselah had been wrong. My concern for others wasn't a bad thing. He hadn't understood that it was the very root of my humanity. That it was as alive as the darkness was. That it wouldn't lead to my downfall at all. Instead, it could—it would—be my salvation, because in it lay my magick.

"Promise me," said Methuselah. *"Promise you will find Grandmother Weaver and save her."*

"I promise."

All that remained of Methuselah turned to ash in my grasp. I turned my hand over and let the fine particles sift through my fingers as, deep in my heart, I said a final farewell to the alien who had been my friend. The heat had nearly reached its zenith, where it would roll out from me and consume all those who the webs had bound. I zeroed in on its nexus with all the focus I could muster.

And then I filled my lungs with air, parted my lips, and slowly—so slowly—exhaled, directing my breath toward it. At first, the stone's heat continued unabated, and unease whispered through me. Had I made a mistake? Been too confident in my capacity to control such power? Then ... then I felt it. The cooling whisper of air across my skin, calm across my mind ... and the tiniest hesitation in the stone.

Symbiosis, I whispered to it. *You help me, and I promise I will find her for you. I will take you to her.*

There was another hesitation, and then, with a suddenness that startled me into a choked inhale, the webs snapped back, detaching from the cocoons in which they'd bound the Mages. Swiftly, before I lost the modicum of control that I seemed to have gained, I focused my gaze on a lump of fabric—a suit jacket—near me. A strand of spider silk slithered toward it, disappeared beneath it, then returned to view with an obsidian stone wrapped inside it.

Certain now of its intent and no longer needing my input, the stone in my palm directed other strands to the remaining three bundles and the lone, uncovered stone still sitting in the middle of the floor. A wail of disappointment mingled with fury came from one of the cocoons. Its occupant was hidden, but the voice belonged to Rebecca, who would no doubt suffer because of this loss. Drummond's puppy would, too.

Perhaps I might have felt a small stab of pity for them if I hadn't just realized my miscalculation. The monumental error I'd made. The sheer catastrophe snaking its way back to me in the form of five spider strands bringing five stones toward the one already embedded in my palm.

Yes, embedded, because at some point one of us had become a little too enthusiastic about this symbiosis thing, and the stone and I—sweet Mary Magdalene—were well and truly bound together now. And, yes, five unprotected, uncovered, bare stones were hurtling to join it.

Us.

And no, there was nothing I could do to stop them.

Hell.

Fucking, fucking—

"Sister Monica!" a voice yelled. "Sister Monica, catch!"

Everything in me paused. Was that—? No. It couldn't be. That was impossible. She was—they were all—

"Sister Monica!" the voice called again, coming from above me. I lifted my head a fraction, seeking the source. And then I saw her leaning over the rail of the balcony over one of the bronze rooms, tall, thin, and holding something aloft as her warm brown gaze met mine across the cocooned Mages.

For an instant, in the space of a heartbeat, my mind jumped back in time to the lawn of the Mary Magdalene House for Women. Back to the beginning of this whole godforsaken—in the most literal sense, it turned out—mess.

"Sister Monica!" a skeletal woman had called from the sagging porch in need of paint. *"This is yours now. Find the others."*

And then she had tossed something to me the way the tall, thin woman did now, and I had summoned a strength and will that I had never imagined I possessed, and I had gathered myself and lunged up from the lawn—or was it the floor— and I had flown through the air and my fingers had closed around the stone—or something soft?—and then—

I grunted as I came down hard on the broken tiles. A jagged edge jabbed into my broken ribs, and pain shafted through me. Not remembered pain, real pain. *Now* pain. Pain that made my eyes tear up and—

I blinked them away as the present snapped back into focus. The shattered lobby, the scattered cocoons in which I'd trapped the Mages—and the returning webs and the stones they brought with them, mere inches away from my bare hand.

"For fucksake, Monica, use the damn shirt!" Talia bellowed.

The air whooshed from me. Talia. I wasn't hallucinating Sister Margaret, I was seeing Talia. The real Talia. And I wasn't at the beginning of this godforsaken mess, I was at the end of it, and the bundle Talia had thrown to me was a shirt, not a rock, and—

"*Monica!*"

Relief bubbled up in my chest, wanting to be a joyous laugh but emerging as a kind of strangled squawk, and I did as I was told.

I used the damn shirt.

CHAPTER 32

Phoenix got to me first, throwing herself at me and knocking me flat, hugging and crying and babbling about nuns and Molotov cocktails and Talia and rented minivans. None of it made sense.

Not her words, not her presence—which I couldn't quite grasp, despite the arms locked around me in an iron grip— and sure as hell not the additional presence of the four Ursulines trying to pick us both up off the floor.

But most of all, not Talia, who swooped down on us, pulled Phoenix briskly to her feet, and began shepherding us deeper into the building in her usual efficient manner.

"We can talk later," she told Phoenix. "Drummond and his minions are still out there somewhere, and the cops will be coming in through that door any second, now that the noise has stopped. We need to find another way out of the building, because we do *not* want to be here. Sister Lise, make sure Sister Colette doesn't fall behind."

"Talia?" I reached out to touch my friend's shoulder, needing to make sure she was real. She slapped my hand away. "Ow!"

She was real, all right. I tipped my head back and laughed in sheer joy—with maybe a little giddiness mixed in. And perhaps a touch of hysteria. I slapped my free hand over my mouth as she glared at me.

"Focus, damn it," she told me. "And walk faster. We can catch up when we're out of here. You sure those things are secure?"

"I'm sure." I hugged my thrice-knotted bundle closer to me and thought about how very fitting it was that Methuselah's shirt carried the stones. Then, when Talia scowled over her shoulder at me, I sped up my steps to match hers, and Phoenix scurried at my side.

Talia had parked the rented minivan in the multilevel parking garage at a mall next to the conference center. It took us the better part of a half hour to get out of the garage and onto the road because of traffic and increased security, but none of us minded. And there was no shortage of conversation to keep us occupied.

We got the story of Talia out of the way first. Phoenix, brilliant tech whiz that she was, had programmed some kind of miraculous image-search-thing to pinpoint the city block from which the photo Rebecca had shown me had likely been taken. There was only one hotel in that block, Phoenix told me—justifiably bursting with pride as she related the story—and the view behind Talia showed that she was somewhere higher up. So the four Ursuline nuns had gone door-to-door, starting on the fourteenth floor and working their way down to the tenth, where door number three had yielded their prize.

"But there were Mages guarding her," I objected. "How——?"

"Sheer surprise with a healthy dose of divine intervention," Sister Bernadette said, taking over the tale. "Plus, Talia's reflexes. There was only one Mage there at the time, and when she realized who we were, she started the whole ... you know"—she made vague rolling motions with her hands in imitation of the Mages' fireball-making—"but Talia grabbed her arms from behind before she could finish. Then Sister Colette ran into her with her walker and knocked her down, and Sister Simonne sat on her while Sister Lise and I held her hands down, and Talia got something to tie her up with."

"Teamwork," Sister Colette added smugly from the back seat of the rented minivan. "That Mage never stood a chance."

Phoenix went back to the story, telling me that there had been no answer when I'd called the monastery because all six of them—Ursulines, Phoenix, and Talia—were already on the road to Ottawa in a rented minivan stocked with Molotovs. They'd used them on the serpent to distract it so they could get inside—and maybe to distract the cops who tried to stop them, too.

"Distract?"

"Distract, threaten," muttered Sister Colette. "Same thing, really."

"Potato, po-*tah*-to," agreed Sister Lise.

"Tomato, to-*mah*-to," added Sister Simonne.

"Oranges and bananas," growled Talia as she signaled for a lane change to take us onto the ramp for the highway. "Distracting and threatening are *not* the same, and we're damned lucky we're not all sitting in cells right now. Or worse."

The nuns, unperturbed and still giddy from their success in rescuing me—because yes, they had done just that— cackled merrily in the two back seats, the normally staid Sister Bernadette included. But Talia's words had reminded me ...

"Lucille!" I shot up straight in the passenger seat beside her. "We have to go back—I have to find Lucille. She—"

"Crashed the semi and was taken to hospital in an ambulance," Talia finished. "We know."

"You—but how?"

"Professional courtesy." Talia pushed down on the gas pedal to pick up speed, checked her side mirror and over her shoulder, and merged left onto Highway 417 East, the first leg of our journey back to the monastery. "I asked the cops at the barricade on our way in, before they"—she jabbed a thumb toward the dark interior behind her—"starting lobbing their firebombs."

"Distractions," Sister Colette replied.

Talia and I both ignored her.

"How badly was she hurt?" I asked, digging my nails into my palms—well, one palm, anyway. I still had to come to terms with the stone fused to the other, but that—that could wait. Lucille could not.

"A couple of bruised ribs and a bump on the head, but apart from that, she was fine."

"But you said ambulance."

Talia shot me a wry, sideways glance. "They were concerned about the heart attack she said she was having—the one that caused her to lose control of her rig."

"Her heart—oh. *Oh.*"

Talia chuckled. "Exactly."

"So, what will happen to her?"

"They'll keep her overnight, probably. Run some tests. Find nothing. Decide it was a panic attack or some such thing." Talia shrugged. "No one was hurt—at least, not by her, so she'll likely just get a slap on the wrist and, given her age, lose her truck license. All in all, not bad."

I turned my head and smiled at my faint reflection in the side window. "She told me that she'd lived a full life," I told Talia. "I'm glad she'll get to live it a little longer."

Talia grunted. "Frankly, I'm glad we all will."

There would be more to talk about later—and far more to worry about, such as Drummond's whereabouts— but for now, it was late, and the adrenaline high was wearing off, and silence settled over all of us. The snow that had fallen earlier, when Lucille and Methuselah and I had come out of the truck stop restaurant, had been cleared from the road, and the van's winter tires hissed over the wet pavement, a low susurration of sound that lulled the tired nuns into sleep within minutes.

I stared out the side window at the buildings and lights flashing by. There were fewer, now. We would be out of the city soon … out of the city and on our way home without him. Without Methuselah and his quirky presence or his sporadic, entirely unreliable, and equally critical gems of knowledge. I inhaled a slow, deep breath.

"Promise me," his memory whispered.

"I promise," I thought back, *"but it would have been so much easier with you to help me."*

Because what now? Where did I even begin? How could I find a mysterious Crone who might or might not be able to help, with nothing more to go on than—

Phoenix's arms slid around my seat from behind and encircled my chest, breaking into my thoughts as she leaned forward to whisper in my ear. "Sister Monica?"

A slow, comfortable warmth flooded me. Sweet Mary Magdalene, I was glad she was safe. I knew I should tell her to put her seatbelt back on, but instead, I put a hand up to cover her linked ones resting on my breastbone. The head of a toy dragon poked out from one of them. I'd found it in the pocket of the shirt I'd wrapped the stones in, when I tucked the bundle under my seat in the van; she'd cried when I'd given it to her.

I cleared the memory from my throat.

"Yes, Phoenix?" I whispered back.

"I found it," she said. "I found the confluence he asked me to look for. It's a town in Ontario. And I think I found who you're supposed to see there, too. Her name is Claire Emerson. The witches call her the Fifth Crone."

Look for more of Sister Monica's story in <u>Return of the Crone</u>, book 6 of the Crone Wars, coming in 2026!

BEHIND THE SCENES

If you happen to live in Ottawa (or have visited), you may recognize the Government Conference Centre as being the current Senate of Canada Building. But it wasn't always the Senate … and it won't always *be* the Senate. Which is why I changed the name for the purposes of this book.

Here's a quick glimpse at the building's history:

Yes, it really was originally built as a passenger train station, and it served as such from 1912 to 1966.

In 1968, the building was converted to the Government Conference Centre, but only a few changes were made to it in the late 1960s and early 1970s.

By 2014, in dire need of an upgrade, it was chosen to be the temporary seat for the Canadian Senate during the long-term restoration of the Parliamentary Precinct (the fancy name for the three enormous buildings that make up Canada's Parliament Hill).

Extensive renovations were undertaken, and the Senate moved to its new accommodation in 2019, where it is expected to remain until work on Centre Block (the main Parliament Hill building) is completed in 2030-2031.

The fate of the Senate of Canada Building is uncertain after that, but according to our lovely young tour guide there (thank you, Luc!), it may once again become the Government Conference Centre.

So … a little bit of creative license, and presto! One name change—and the elimination of a *whole* lot of additional, very complicated security—later, the Government Conference Centre is where Sister Monica and her friends make their last stand. For now, *wink, wink*.

Other fun facts (because research!) about the building:

There was a heavy focus on "green" building during construction, with workers reusing or repurposing as much of the heritage material as they could. Ninety percent of the construction waste was diverted from landfill, and energy-efficient plumbing, lighting, heating, and insulation were installed.

Bees! Thirteen hives were installed beside the Senate of Canada building, each marked by one of the provincial/territorial flags, and 100,000 honeybees moved in alongside the senators in 2019. The bees help pollinate parks and gardens, the hives are maintained by a local beekeeper, and the population is expected to grow up to 650,000.

And yes, I think that last fact was my favourite.

Also By

The Obsidian Sisterhood

A Web of Obsidian

A Tangle of Obsidian

The Crone Wars

Becoming Crone

A Gathering of Crones

Game of Crones

Crone Unleashed

Rise of the Crones

The Grigori Legacy

Sins of the Angels (Grigori Legacy book 1)

Sins of the Son (Grigori Legacy book 2)

Sins of the Lost (Grigori Legacy book 3)

Sins of the Warrior (Grigori Legacy book 4)

Other Books by Linda Poitevin

The Ever After Romance Collection

Gwynneth Ever After

Forever After

Forever Grace

Always and Forever

Abigail Always

Shadow of Doubt

ACKNOWLEDGEMENTS

I think the list of people I want to thank grows longer with each and every story that I write. It's a good problem to have, despite my fear of accidentally leaving someone out! The bulk of my gratitude goes, as always, to my husband and family, for their unwavering support and understanding—especially when deadlines are breathing down my neck and I become somewhat inaccessible … to say the least—and to Marie Bilodeau, the bestest writing friend ever.

Huge thanks again to my fantastic support team, too: Laura Paquet, copy editor; Erica Ball, proofreader; Author Tree, interior layout; and Deranged Doctor Design, cover art. My stories are made better (and more beautiful) because of their hard work.

Special thanks also goes out to new beta readers Joann Longo, Hope O'Keefe, Rhonda Pierson Foote, and Suzanne Segady for their fantastic feedback on Sister Monica's newest adventure, and to my amazing agent Sara Megibow, audio publisher Insatiable Press, and narrator Senn Annis for helping to bring Monica to life through audio.

And if I've forgotten you in this list, it's not because I don't love and appreciate you, it's because some days, I can't remember my *own* name, lol. Believe me, I am acutely aware of how much I owe to so many … and I am eternally grateful.

About The Author

Lydia M. Hawke is a pseudonym used by me, Linda Poitevin, for my urban fantasy books. Together, we are the author of books that range from supernatural suspense thrillers to contemporary romances and romantic suspense.

Originally from beautiful British Columbia, I moved to Canada's capital region of Ottawa-Gatineau more than thirty years ago with the love of my life. Which means I've been married most of my life now, and I've spent most of it here. Wow. Anyway, when I'm not plotting the world's downfall or next great love story, I'm also a wife, mom, grandma, friend, walker of a Giant Dog, keeper of many cats, and an avid gardener and food preserver. My next great ambition in life (other than writing the next book, of course) is to have an urban chicken coop. Yes, seriously…because chickens.

You can find me hanging out on Facebook at facebook.com/LydiaMHawke, and on my website at LydiaHawkeBooks.com, where you can also join my newsletter for updates on new books (and a free story!)

I love to hear from readers and can be reached at lydia@lydiahawkebooks.com. And yes, I answer all my emails!